THROUGH THE FLAMES

LEFT BEHIND

>THE KIDS<

Jerry B. Jenkins

Tim LaHaye

TYNDALE HOUSE PUBLISHERS, INC.
WHEATON, ILLINOIS

Visit Tyndale's exciting Web site at www.tyndale.com

Discover the latest Left Behind news at www.leftbehind.com

Published in association with the literary agency of Alive Communications, Inc., 7680 Goddard Street, Suite 200, Colorado Springs, CO 80920.

Designed by Brian Eterno
Edited by Rick Blanchette

ISBN 0-8423-2195-0

Printed in the United States of America

05 04 03 02 01
25 24 23 22 21 20 19

To Ryan Thompson
Welcome to the family of God

Contents

ONE

A Line in the Sand

JUDD Thompson and the other three kids living in his otherwise abandoned suburban house sometimes felt as if it was just them against the world. Judd, at sixteen, was the oldest. Then came the redhead, Vicki Byrne, a year younger. Lionel Washington was thirteen, and Ryan Daley, twelve.

They were the only ones left from their families. Judd's parents and his twin younger brother and sister had disappeared right out of their clothes a few days before. Vicki Byrne, who had lived in a trailer park with her parents and little sister, had seen the same thing happen at her place. Her older brother, who had moved to Michigan, had disappeared too, according to one of his friends.

Lionel Washington had lost his parents,

his older sister, and his little brother and sister. His uncle, the infamous André Dupree, was thought dead, but Lionel now knew he was alive somewhere—but where?

Ryan Daley had been an only child, and now he was an orphan. His parents had not disappeared. They had died in separate accidents related to the worldwide vanishings of millions of people—his father in a plane crash, his mother in an explosion while in her car.

The kids knew what had happened. At least the three older ones did. Ryan wasn't sure yet. All he knew was that he had been left alone in the world, and he didn't much like the explanation the other three had come to believe.

All three of the older kids had had parents who were Christians. They believed not only in God, but also in Christ. And they weren't just churchgoers. These were people who had believed that the way to God, the way to heaven, was through Christ. In other words, they did not agree with so many people who believed that if you just tried to live right and be good and treat other people fairly, you could earn your way to heaven and to favor with God.

As logical as all that may have sounded, the parents of Judd and Vicki and Lionel believed that the real truth, the basic teaching of the New Testament, was summarized in two verses in the book of Ephesians. Chapter 2, verses 8-9 said that a person is saved by grace through faith and that it is not as a result of anything we accomplished. It is the gift of God, not a result of good deeds, so nobody can brag about it.

They also believed that one day, as the Bible also foretold, Jesus would return and snatch true believers away in the twinkling of an eye, and they would immediately join him in heaven. That was what had happened, Judd, Vicki, and Lionel realized, since most of the people in their churches had disappeared too.

But what convinced them more than anything was that they themselves were still here. Judd had never received Christ, though he had grown up in church and knew the Bible. Vicki had hated it when her parents had become Christians two years before, and she didn't want anything to do with it, even though her older brother and younger sister had also believed. She had seen the changes in her family and realized there was some truth to what was going on. She had an idea they were onto something real, but she wasn't willing to give up her lifestyle or her freedom to join them in their faith.

Lionel had been more like Judd, having been raised by a Christian family and having gone to church every Sunday for years. He had not become a rebel as Judd did when he became a teenager. Rather, he had pretended all along to be a Christian. It was his and his uncle André's secret. They were not really Christians.

Those oldest three kids realized their tragic mistake immediately when the vanishings had taken place. In the midst of chaos, as cars crashed, planes fell from the sky, ships collided and sank, houses burned, and people panicked, they had to admit they had been wrong—as wrong as people could be. They were glad to find out there was a second chance for them, that they could still come to Christ. But though that gave them the assurance that they would one day see God and be reunited with their families, it didn't keep them from grieving over the loss of their loved ones. They were alone in the world until they had discovered each other and Bruce Barnes, the visitation pastor at New Hope Village Church who had agreed to help teach them the Bible. He had given them each a Bible and invited them to the first Sunday service following the disappearances, which the Bible predicted centuries ago.

But Ryan Daley was still a holdout. He was

scared. He was sad. He was angry. And while he had been hanging with Lionel since they had met, Lionel made him feel like a wimp. Well, he didn't just *feel* like one. He *was* one. Lionel seemed brave. He confronted his uncle's enemies, he had been to the morgue to try to identify his uncle's body, and he had gone into Ryan's house after a burglary. Ryan couldn't force himself to do any of that stuff, and it made him feel terrible.

Judd had invited everybody to live at his place. Vicki didn't have any choice after her trailer had burned to the ground. Some of Lionel's uncle André's "associates" had virtually taken over Lionel's place, so he needed somewhere to crash too. Ryan could have stayed at his own house and Lionel would have stayed there with him, but Ryan couldn't make himself go inside. There were too many scary memories. It had been just him and his parents in that house, and now they were dead. And then there had been the burglary, so he wasn't about to set foot in the place. Lionel could make fun of him all he wanted, but Ryan was glad to take Judd up on his offer.

Judd's family had clearly been the wealthiest of the four. His house was a huge mansion. Well, almost a mansion. There were bigger and nicer homes around, but not many. In Judd's house, each kid could have his own bedroom and lots of privacy.

No one knew what the future held, at least among the kids. Bruce Barnes sure seemed to know. He had made it his business to become a student of Bible prophecy and must have been spending almost every spare minute buried in the Bible and reference books. He told the kids that it was time to be on the lookout for a man the Bible called the Antichrist. "He will come offering peace and harmony, and many people will be fooled, thinking he's a good man with their best interests at heart. He will make some sort of an agreement with the nation of Israel, but it will be a lie. The signing of that agreement will signal the beginning of the last seven years of tribulation before Christ returns again to set up his thousand-year kingdom on earth."

Bruce explained the Tribulation as a period of suffering for all the people of the world, more suffering even than they had endured when millions of people had disappeared all at the same time. Bruce promised to teach the kids all of the judgments that would come from heaven during those seven years, some twenty-one of them in three series of seven.

Judd had called the kids together one

evening after they had all received their Bibles from Bruce. "I'm not trying to be the boss or anything," he began, "but I am the oldest and this is my house, and so there are going to be some rules. To stay in this house, we all have to agree to watch out for each other. Let each other know where you are all the time so we don't worry about you. Don't do anything stupid like getting in trouble, breaking the law, staying out all night, that kind of stuff. And I think we all ought to be reading what Bruce tells us to read every day and also going to whatever meetings he invites us to, besides church of course. I mean, we're going to church every Sunday to keep up with what's going on."

Vicki and Lionel nodded. "Of course," Vicki said. "Sounds fair."

"Not to me," Ryan said. "I'm not into this stuff, and you all know it."

"Guess you're going to have to live somewhere else then," Lionel said.

"That's not for you to say, Lionel!" Ryan said. "This isn't your house! Judd's not going to make me read the Bible and go to church meetings just to stay here. Are you, Judd?"

"Matter of fact, I am," Judd said.

"What?"

"I can hardly believe I'm saying this," Judd said, "because just last week it made me so mad when my parents said the same thing. But here goes. As long as you live under my roof, you follow my rules."

Ryan's face was red, and it appeared he might bolt out of there like he often did when he heard something he didn't like.

"I'm not going to force you to become a Christian," Judd said. "Nobody can do that. Even Vicki and I needed to decide that in our own time on our own terms. But I'm taking you in, man. You're staying here because I asked you to. The least you can do is to join in with what the rest of us are doing. It's all for one and one for all. We're going to look out for you and protect you and take care of you, even if you don't believe like we do, and we're going to expect you to do the same for us. I can't even make you read the Bible, but we're going to go to church and to Bruce's special little meetings, and we're going together. You can plug your ears or sleep through them, but you're going."

"And if I don't?"

"Then you can find someplace else to stay."

"He'll never do that," Lionel said. "He's too much of a scaredy-cat."

"Shut up!" Ryan said.

"Lay off him, Lionel," Vicki said. "You're not going to win him over that way."

"You're not going to win me over at all," Ryan said. "Just watch."

"Well," Judd said, "what's the deal. You in or out?"

"I have to decide right now?"

"We have a meeting with Bruce tonight and church tomorrow morning. You go with us tonight and you promise to go tomorrow, or you move out this afternoon."

"The man's drawing a line in the sand for you," Lionel said.

"Lionel!" Vicki scolded.

"I'm just sayin', the line has been drawn. You crossing the line, Ryan? Or are you with us?"

"I'll think about it," Ryan said, and he was gone. The others heard him banging around in the bedroom he had been assigned.

"We need to pray for him," Vicki said. "It's hard enough for us, but imagine what it's like for him. We know where our parents are. If he believes like we do that our parents were raptured and his weren't, he has to accept that his parents are in hell. Think about that. He's going to fight this a long time, because even if he wants to become a believer, that means he's accepting that his parents are lost forever."

"It sure would be nice if we could somehow find out his parents, or at least one of them, was actually a Christian or became one before they died," Lionel said.

"Get real," Judd said. "That rarely happens in real life."

"I know."

Lionel was dealing with his own dilemma. His uncle had left a long message on Lionel's answering machine, going on and on about killing himself and feeling so bad that he had influenced Lionel to not be a Christian. He was clearly drunk or high or both, and Lionel had been convinced that André had killed himself. When Lionel and Ryan had ridden their bikes all the way to André's neighborhood one night to investigate, the cops had told them André's body was at a nearby morgue. It had indeed been a suicide, they told Lionel. Because André, had had enemies to whom he owed money, and those guys had moved into Lionel's house and kicked him out, Lionel figured they had murdered André and made it look like suicide.

But when Judd had driven Lionel to the morgue a few days later so Lionel could identify the body, he had run into a shocker. While the victim was the same height and weight as André, and while he had carried André's wallet and wore André's clothes and jewelry, the body was clearly not André's.

Finding the truth about that mystery

would be Lionel's mission over the next several days. Meanwhile, he was as eager as Judd and Vicki to learn more about what life was supposed to be like, now that Christ had raptured his church.

Judd agreed that they should pray for Ryan, and that in fact they should pray at the end of all their little house meetings, the way Bruce had them pray at the end of their meetings at church. But first he asked, "Is there anything else either of you needs to talk about now?"

"Yeah," Lionel said. "I just want to say that I'm not really trying to put down Ryan. I'm trying to toughen him up the way I did my little brother and sister and the way my sister did me. I don't want to make him mad or feel bad, but he's such a wuss. It's time for that boy to grow up."

"It's hard to grow up this way," Vicki said. "I don't know about you guys, but I'm having trouble. I have bad dreams, have trouble sleeping, find myself crying over my family as if they're all just dead and gone and not in heaven where I know I'll see them someday. I know we're all going to be called back to school one of these days, and I can't imagine sitting through class with all I know now. If this Antichrist guy shows up soon and does sign some sort of a contract with Israel, we're gonna have only seven more years to live."

Judd and Lionel sat nodding. "Anyway," Judd said, "Lionel, you do have to try to encourage Ryan. If he decides against becoming a Christian, I sure wouldn't want to have it on my conscience that I pushed him away. As much as you guys squabble, I still think he looks up to you."

"Really?"

"Oh, yeah," Vicki said. "I think that's obvious. He wants your approval."

"Wow."

"You might want to encourage him."

"Hold up," Lionel said. "I'll do it right now."

Lionel hurried to Ryan's room, trying to decide what to say. When he peeked in and knocked, Ryan whirled from what he was doing.

"Hey, little man," Lionel said.

"I thought I asked you to quit calling me that," Ryan said.

"Yeah, sorry. Listen, I just want to say that I'm sorry about getting on your case all the time."

Ryan didn't respond.

Lionel tried again. "I mean, uh, I'm just saying—"

Ryan approached the door, where Lionel

stood, tongue-tied. "You're just saying you don't know what you're saying, right?"

Lionel did not respond.

"Are you finished?" Ryan asked, his hand on the door.

"No, I—"

"Yes, you are," Ryan said. And he pushed the door shut in Lionel's face.

Lionel returned to Judd and Vicki, clearly troubled. He told them what had happened.

"We do need to pray for that boy," Vicki said.

But before they did, Lionel said, "You need to know he was packing up."

"Really?" Judd said. "He's leaving?"

"I don't know," Lionel said, "but he was getting all his stuff together."

And they prayed for him.

TWO

Ryan's Escapade

RYAN was angry and confused. What else could he be? He had overheard Vicki trying to explain his situation, and she was exactly right. In truth, he wanted to believe exactly what these other kids believed. It all made sense. His friend, Raymie Steele, had warned him. And it seemed most of the people who had disappeared were known to be Christians. So many people from so many churches were gone that they must have known something.

But if all this was true, his parents had not made it. But still they were gone. Dead. The only nightmare worse than having your parents die, Ryan decided, was knowing that they had missed going to heaven. Was that fair? What kind of a God did something like that to people as nice as his parents? Or to someone like him?

He wasn't a bad kid. Sure, he had done a lot of things wrong, but who hadn't? Raymie Steele was a Christian, but he wasn't perfect.

The one thing Ryan couldn't get out of his mind was that if this was true and his parents knew it, they would have believed. And for sure they would want him to believe before it was too late. But knowing it was probably true, even believing it, didn't mean Ryan was accepting it for himself. Because what Vicki Byrne had said was right. If he bought into it, it meant he was admitting that his parents had missed out and were in hell. That was too much to take in just now.

Ryan knew something the other kids didn't know. Well, except maybe Lionel. Lionel seemed to know Ryan better than Ryan knew himself. What only Ryan, and maybe Lionel, knew was that Ryan had no intention of doing anything that would cause him to leave Judd's house. He had never felt or been so alone in his life, and these kids were his new family. Whether or not he became a Christian, he was not about to leave them or let them abandon him.

Yeah, they treated him like a baby and used names for him that made him feel even smaller and younger. But he *had* been acting like a baby. He had a right. He was an orphan. The others were enduring the loss of their families too, but this was different. Ryan needed time away from the pressure, time to think, time to do something to take his mind off everything. He had to admit he was afraid to go out alone at night, so while it was still light, he headed out on his bike.

The others had seemed so concerned with his packing up his stuff that they would likely watch to see if he took it with him. They would be relieved, he hoped, to find everything still in his room. It was packed and stacked, though, so they could wonder if he was eventually going to leave, based on what decision he came to. But his decision, at least about staying at Judd's, was already made.

It made Ryan feel a little better to know that the others seemed to want him to stay regardless. He knew they wanted him to become a Christian, but that didn't seem to have anything to do with whether he stayed around. Was it because they really cared for him? Were they actually worried about him and looking out for him? He couldn't figure that one out. He had never cared about anybody else that much, except maybe Raymie.

Ryan wanted to work on his courage. Could he ride into his own neighborhood and past his own house? And if he could, could he also see what was happening at the

Steeles'? He sure didn't want to ask them about Mrs. Steele or Raymie, because he knew both Mr. Steele and Raymie's big sister Chloe had to feel terrible about their vanishing. Maybe they'd be like his aunt was a few years ago, who seemed to want to do nothing more than talk about Ryan's uncle at his uncle's funeral. That seemed so strange. You'd think she would have been so upset she wouldn't want his name even mentioned. But she had talked about him nonstop. She even asked people to tell her their favorite stories about him.

"Sit here with me for a minute," she had said, taking Ryan's hand. "Tell me about that time your uncle Walter was trying to teach you to fish and he fell into the lake."

"Oh, Aunt Evelyn," Ryan had said, feeling sheepish and awkward. "You know Uncle Wally did that on purpose. I mean, I was only eight, but I knew that even then."

Aunt Evelyn had leaned back in her chair and laughed her hearty laugh, right there in the funeral home with people filing past the body of her husband. Many turned to stare at the insensitive person who would be guffawing at a time like that and were at first shocked, then pleased to find it was Aunt Evelyn herself.

"I saw the whole thing from the porch of

the cottage," she had said, wiping away her tears of laughter. Ryan thought it funny that she usually cried when she laughed, but of course maybe this time she was covering her real tears of sadness. "I just knew what he was going to do because he had done it to me when we were first dating. He stepped on one side of the boat and then the other, and he kept saying, 'No problem. No problem. Shouldn't stand up in the boat, but don't you worry, I've got it all under control.' Right? Right? Didn't he say that in that big phony deep voice of his?"

"Yes, he did," Ryan had admitted.

"And then, pretending to adjust the fishing line or something, he just stepped back and flipped over the side in his shirt and pants and hat and everything. Didn't he?"

"Yeah, but he had put his glasses in the picnic basket first, and he even took out his hearing aid."

That just made Aunt Evelyn laugh all the more, and soon everyone in the room was waiting his turn to tell a favorite Uncle Walter story. Just thinking about that crazy funeral made Ryan pedal harder as he sped toward his own block. Aunt Evelyn herself had died not two years later. How he missed them both!

Why, he wondered, was he thinking about

them now? Maybe because it reminded him that Raymie Steele had not been the first person to ever tell him about God. Ryan had been to Vacation Bible School a couple of times, but it was at Uncle Walter's funeral, when Ryan had worked up the courage to ask Aunt Evelyn why she wasn't more sad, that she had said that confusing thing to him.

"That's an excellent question, Ryan honey," she had said. She almost always would call him that, even in front of other people. "I'm sad and I'll have my bad days and nights, and I'll cry enough tears for the whole family. But you see, I know where Uncle Walter is, and it's where I'm going to be someday. He's in heaven."

"But how do you know?"

"The Bible says you can know," she had said.

But that was as far as the conversation had gone. Ryan had thought about that a long time and even asked his mom and dad about it. Uncle Walter was Mr. Daley's much older brother, and Aunt Evelyn was his second wife. "Your dad says your uncle Walter's wife has always been some kind of a religious nut, Ryan," his mother had said. "But she means well. She's been good for Walter."

"Good for him?" Mr. Daley had chimed in. "Took all the fun out of him, if you ask me.

Got him the old-time religion, and he became a Holy Joe."

"He was still fun, Dad," Ryan had said. "He was always being funny."

"He kept telling us we need Jesus," Mr. Daley said. "But frankly, I don't feel the need for anything."

Ryan skidded to a stop in front of Raymie Steele's house. He couldn't tell whether Mr. Steele and Chloe were home. So that was it, he realized about his thoughts turning to his uncle Walter and aunt Evelyn. They had been Christians. They were in heaven. And they had tried to tell him and his parents about Christ. He wondered how many other chances his parents had had. His dad always had some comment when he saw a preacher on television. He thought they were all crooks, but he never kept the TV channel on any church program long enough to hear what they had to say.

Ryan sat straddling his bike, pawing the ground with his foot. What he wouldn't give to have it be just a week or so ago and to know that Raymie would come bounding out of this house for some fun. Man, they had good times. They squabbled and argued and had often been jealous of each other, but not a day went by when they didn't have more fun than any two kids deserved. They were best friends, blood brothers, and had pledged to always keep in touch—no matter where college or life took them. How Ryan wanted to see Raymie again!

He pedaled slowly to the end of the block, where his house came into view. There was a pile of newspapers on the stoop, and he knew he should get rid of them and call to cancel the paper. Making it obvious no one was home was an invitation to more burglaries. The drapes were all shut, too. And though there were lights on an automatic timer, all the power outages lately put them on a crazy schedule. The lights were on now and would go off early in the evening. Ryan thought about going in and resetting the timer and opening the drapes so it looked like the house was lived in. But as usual, he couldn't force himself to even move up the driveway by himself, let alone approach the front door. What in the world was he going to do when the lawn needed mowing?

Ryan headed off to the other side of town, where Lionel had lived. He would be scared to death to approach that house with all of André Dupree's so-called friends living there. But still, he wanted to see it, to spy on it. He couldn't figure out what was happening with Lionel's uncle André.

Ryan had been there when Lionel had

played the answering machine message from André. He had to agree, the guy sounded ready to kill himself. Lionel was only kidding himself, Ryan thought, to think that someone André owed money to had killed him and made it look like suicide. The two guys Lionel said had threatened André once were the leaders of the bunch that had moved into Lionel's house, supposedly with André's permission. And they talked about how great it would be when André joined them. How did that make sense, especially now that Lionel had discovered that whoever had been killed in André's apartment, in André's clothes, wearing André's jewelry, and carrying André's wallet, was not André at all?

Ryan was as curious as he could be, but on the other hand, he wasn't sure he wanted to know. What would he do with that information?

He looked at his watch. He knew Judd Thompson had been serious, and that if Ryan was not back at Judd's house and ready to go to the meeting with Bruce that night, he would no longer be welcome. He still had an hour. Ryan rode idly up and down the sidewalk on the other side of the street from Lionel's. There was little going on at the house across the street, but the van was there and lights were on in the house.

At one side of the house was a wide driveway that served the home next door. No one seemed to be home there. Ryan wondered if he would be noticed if he parked his bike out of sight and just moseyed over there, appearing to just be hanging around, playing. That would be a test of his courage, wouldn't it? He didn't think anyone in Lionel's house would recognize him as the one who had sped away from there on bikes with Lionel. And if anyone didn't want him playing in that area next to the house, he'd just move along.

The plan sounded reasonable to Ryan, but he found himself petrified when he actually began walking across the street. He wasn't sure why he was doing this, except that he was hoping to take some bit of information back to Lionel. Maybe Lionel would respect him if he actually did something grown-up, something brave. Plus he really wanted to be helpful. He figured Lionel would rather live with the others at Judd's anyway, but it wasn't right to be driven out of your own home for no reason.

The police were too busy with all the other emergencies to be worried about something like this, but what if he and Lionel took them solid evidence on the fake suicide? It had obviously been a murder. If the police could be convinced of that, maybe Lionel's invaded house would wind up higher on their list of what needed to be investigated.

But what if it had been André who had committed the murder? Who else could have gotten into his place and put all his stuff on another person before killing him? Ryan was beginning to think he was in over his head.

Worse, he felt conspicuous walking across the street. He knew no one noticed or cared, but he felt as if every eye on the street was on him. Just putting one foot in front of the other took all the concentration he could muster. He tried to look casual, as if he were just strolling nowhere.

When he finally reached the driveway between the houses, he moved toward the back so he would be out of sight. He settled on the grass at the far back corner of Lionel's house, close to the neighbor's house and as far away from Lionel's garage as he could be and still be on Lionel's property. He was afraid someone might see him from the window, so he crept up to the wall and sat with his back to the foundation. The cold cement made him shiver, but he knew he was close enough now that if someone looked out a window, he wouldn't be seen.

What was he doing, he wondered? Putting himself in danger just to prove that he could?

What good would he be to anyone if he was discovered? And what might these characters do to him? Would they hurt him? Kidnap him? Kill him? And if they did, where would he be then?

That was something he had to think about as he sat there in the grass, a couple of blades of it in his hands. He pulled the thin green strips apart and smelled the richness of the ground beneath him. It was one thing to hold out on his own decision about God because he didn't like what had happened to his parents. But what would they want for him if this was the truth?

How would he ever see Raymie again, or Aunt Evelyn and Uncle Walter? He knew he was still here because he had heard the truth and not acted on it. How long was he going to be stubborn, hoping everyone else was wrong when he knew full well they were right?

Maybe tonight, maybe at the meeting, he would ask to stay after and talk to Bruce. He didn't want to do something just because everybody wanted him to. He wouldn't be pressured into this. But he still had a lot of questions, and if anyone knew the answers, it would be Bruce.

Ryan froze when he heard footsteps above

him in the house. He wasn't about to stand and peer into a window. He held his breath.

There was the squeak of a bedspring, as if someone had sat on the bed. He heard a mechanical sound he didn't recognize, but it came to him when he heard one end of a conversation. Someone had placed a phone call. It was a woman, sitting on the bed in the room just above him. He was able to hear her clearly if he kept his breathing shallow.

"André," she was saying, "you ought not to be drinkin' now. You got to keep yourself healthy, and you can surface sometime soon."

Surface? Ryan wondered. *What does that mean? He's hiding out somewhere but he can come out soon? Will he have a disguise? He'd have to have a new name. Did the police even suspect that he was still alive, that they had assumed the wrong dead man was André?*

"Now don't you go gettin' religious on me now, hon. You're just lonely. . . . Your cousin was over here the other day, and the guys offered to let him stay. But he wasn't too happy about us being here and he took off. . . . Yes, someone will try to find out where he is and check up on him. Or you can do that yourself in a few days. But you've got to be careful now, you hear? . . . No! Now don't be worrying about him. It wasn't your fault. He seems like a smart kid who can take care of himself. . . . Thirteen?! Are you sure? That big gangly boy? He looked sixteen if he was a minute. Well, he spoke well for himself—even stood up to the guys here. Don't worry about him. . . . Quit your crying now. This will all be over soon. . . . I love you, so shut up."

Ryan jumped to his feet and ran down the driveway and across the street to his bike. He had done his job. He had accomplished something. He had something to tell the others. André was alive. André was in hiding. André would be coming out into the open soon and might even come to Lionel's house.

But what was all that stuff about André getting religious and worrying about Lionel? His phone message that night must have been real. He must have really been worried about what his influence had meant to Lionel. That had to be good news, right?

Ryan began pedaling back toward Judd's when the door of Lionel's house burst open and a thin, young black woman raced at him across the lawn. Had she been the one on the phone? Had she seen him? What did she want?

Ryan tried to accelerate, but he couldn't do it fast enough. The woman overtook him and grabbed him by the shoulders. For as thin as she looked, she was wiry and muscular, much stronger than Ryan. The bike stopped beneath him, and it was all he could do to stay upright.

"What were you doing in our yard?" she demanded.

"*Your* yard?" Ryan said, barely able to catch his breath. His heart banged so hard in his chest that he worried his ribs would crack "I thought it was my friend's yard."

"And who is your friend?"

Ryan knew better than to say. He kept his mouth shut.

"Maybe you'd like to tell one of the men in my house."

Ryan was petrified. "I'm not going to tell anybody anything," he said, amazed that had come out of his mouth. What he wanted to do, what he was afraid he would do, was break down and cry and tell everything. He was a friend of Lionel's, and Lionel wanted his house back, but that news would bring all kinds of trouble down on Ryan and his friends.

"We'll just see about that," the woman said. She strengthened her grip on Ryan's shoulders and began to yank him off his bike.

"You don't have to do that," Ryan lied. "I'll

come with you. I'm not afraid of you or anyone in my friend's house."

"Then get off that bike and come in here."

She kept one hand on his arm as Ryan dismounted, and he noticed one of the men of the house coming out onto the front porch. If that guy joined her, he was in trouble.

As he climbed off his bike, she let go of his arm and the man on the porch hollered out, "You need help, Talia?"

"No! He's comin', and you're gonna talk to him!"

But with that, Ryan pulled away and began running with all his might, pushing his bike along. The woman yelled at him and took out after him, but Ryan was fast. He didn't want to jump on his bike until he knew he had enough speed to get away from her. She was yelling for the man on the porch. "LeRoy! Get him!"

"Get him?" LeRoy shouted back with a laugh. "I'll run him down!"

Ryan was sprinting as fast as he could and sensed he was pulling away from Talia when he heard the old rattletrap van start up. He leapt onto his bike and pedaled with all his might. His only hope, he knew, was that his bike could go places that van couldn't. And Ryan knew this suburb.

It wasn't long before Talia had quit running because she fell too far behind. But Ryan could hear that old van engine growling, and he was scared to death.

He cut through yards, went down alleys, turned every which way as fast as he could. He thought he had gotten away from LeRoy a couple of times, and then he showed up, somehow guessing where Ryan would come out. LeRoy never got closer than a block or so, though, until Ryan got into his own neighborhood. LeRoy was about a block behind and closing fast when Ryan got near Raymie Steele's house. Raymie and Ryan had a route they always used when going between their houses, especially when they were trying to sneak somewhere or were trying to keep from being seen. It went through the side of Raymie's yard to the back and through the hedges in his yard to the hedges of the next one. That led into an alley that emptied out right near Ryan's house.

It put him right in plain sight unless he got there fast enough that no one was right behind him. If someone came out of that alley late enough and couldn't see him, he wouldn't know which way Ryan had turned. Actually, he didn't turn at all. Ryan just made a jog around the side of his own house and slipped through a small cutout in the fence.

He usually ran through the shortcut, but on his bike he was really flying.

When he got to Raymie's side yard, his bike fishtailed in the grass, but he couldn't slow down. He just tried to stay up while still pedaling fast. He straightened out just in time to squeeze through those two hedges, but he could see LeRoy and his van heading for the alley. LeRoy had to slow down to make the turn, and by that time Ryan was through the hedges and clear. He could hear LeRoy but he couldn't see him, so he knew LeRoy couldn't see him either.

Ryan shot through the lawn at the side of his house, riding as fast as he ever had. His legs were burning, and he was gasping. He saw the headlights of the van just as he got to the fence and knew if he got off his bike and tried to slither through the fence on foot, LeRoy would see his bike and know where he was.

He had to take a chance. He was afraid he was going to tear himself up, but he remembered that he had gotten in trouble with his dad the last time he crawled through that opening in the chain-link fence—he had made the hole wider, and his dad had said Ryan was going to have to work with him when he fixed it. But they had never gotten around to it. He was going full speed next to that fence, hoping LeRoy would not find him with his headlights. Ryan put the bike down, and it slid through the grass, over to the fence, and right through the opening. Ryan felt the fence brush the back of his head, but it did not draw blood. The back wheel got hung up in the fence, and he tumbled off into the backyard. He dragged the bike far enough around the back so no one could see him, and ran into the house.

The last thing he wanted to do was go inside his own house, but what else could he do? All of a sudden that scary house looked like the safest place he knew. He didn't turn on any lights. He just lay on the floor in the kitchen in the dark and tried to catch his breath so he could hear which way the van went. He heard LeRoy racing up and down the street, as if he was sure Ryan had to be there somewhere. Luckily for Ryan, the light timer didn't kick on and give him away. LeRoy finally drove off.

Ryan shakily crept to the phone and called Bruce.

THREE

The Meeting

IT WAS time for Judd, Vicki, Lionel, and Ryan to drive to the church for their private meeting with Bruce Barnes. Judd kept looking at his watch, wondering how long he should wait for Ryan.

"Maybe he's not coming," Lionel said. "Maybe he's made his decision."

"You know him better than that," Vicki said. "You know he wouldn't even want to be out after dark."

"That means he found another place to stay," Lionel said. "Or he talked himself into going back to his own house."

"He'll go crazy there alone," Vicki said.

Judd couldn't believe how disappointed he was that Ryan was not back. He vowed he would wait five more minutes, and that would be it. "If he's not here when we leave," Judd said, "he's out."

"But what if he shows up at church?" Vicki said.

"Unlikely. But if he does, he'd better have a good story."

Judd broke his own vow and waited ten more minutes. He shook his head and pulled his jacket on. Vicki said, "Judd, I have a bad feeling about this."

"So do I, Vicki, but I made an ultimatum and I have to stick to it."

"No you don't. We're not about ultimatums. We're about mercy and grace, like Bruce always says."

Judd hesitated. At first he was angry that she was trying to correct him. Was she trying to take over? But then he thought, *Who cares who's in charge anyway, just because I'm older and it's my house?* Actually, he wanted a way out of this.

Vicki continued. "You said yourself that we were to watch out for each other. All for one and one for all. I mean, if he had come back here and told us to our faces that he wanted out, that he refused to play by our rules, then fine. He's never been afraid to speak his mind. He wouldn't leave and not say anything. Anyway, he has to come back sometime to get his stuff."

Judd knew she was right. "But why didn't

he call? He knows he's risking getting kicked out of the house."

"I'm afraid he's in some kind of trouble," she said.

"I could be wrong," Lionel said, "but I think he's too chicken to get himself into trouble. That kid wouldn't go with me into his own house in broad daylight."

"He knows you think that too," Vicki said. "Maybe he went and did something foolish to try to prove himself to you."

"I doubt it," Lionel said. "I told you he just blew me off when I tried to apologize."

"So he doesn't know how to accept an apology. Is that a crime? He didn't have any brothers or sisters, and you can bet his parents didn't apologize to him much."

Judd was beginning to think Vicki was onto something. "So, if we're going to look out for him," he said, "where do we start? Where was he going?"

"I have no idea," Lionel said, and Vicki shrugged too.

"He was on his bike," Judd said. "Let's just drive around Mount Prospect and take the long way to the church."

"Should we call Bruce?" Vicki said. "Tell him we're going to be a little late?"

There she went again with suggestions, Judd thought. But again, she was probably right. He wasn't used to catering to adults like Bruce. Respecting people was something new for him, and, he knew, for her too. "My dad's car has a phone in it," he said. "That'll save us some time."

They piled into the car, and Judd dialed the church as he drove. Loretta, Bruce's secretary, answered in her southern accent. She said Bruce was on the phone. Judd told her his problem. "Why, young man, I believe Ryan is the one on the phone with Pastor Barnes right now."

"Where was he calling from?"

"I don't rightly know. Shall I have Bruce call you when he's free?"

"No, thanks. Just tell him we're on our way."

That was encouraging, at least. Judd hated the thought of Ryan having called his bluff and making him follow through on his ultimatum. Ryan reminded Judd so much of himself at that age. Judd had been in a church family, of course, but it was late in his twelfth year that he began to become rebellious. A rage had grown inside him that he didn't understand. He saw some of that in Ryan, and he didn't want him to run from the group. Ryan needed them. And they wanted him.

"I begged Ryan to tell me where he was,"

Bruce said a few minutes later. "He sounded really scared. All he said was to tell you, Judd, that he would get to the meeting as soon as the coast was clear."

"'The coast was clear'?" Judd said. "What in the world is he talking about?"

"I told him I'd come and get him, wherever he is, but he said he doesn't want me leading anybody to him, whatever that means."

Judd could see from the looks on the others' faces that they were as dumbfounded as he was.

"I've got a lot I want to tell you tonight," Bruce said, "and I'd like Ryan to hear it. But I've had a long day and don't want to be up till all hours like I have been the last two nights. Should we get started, and then you can bring Ryan up-to-date when he gets here?"

That sounded good to Judd, but Vicki said, "I don't know if I can concentrate while I'm worrying about Ryan."

"I think he's safe," Bruce said, "as scared and mysterious as he sounded. Let's try to get something accomplished and not just spend our time worrying. Be praying for him, but let me teach you some things."

Bruce spent about half an hour going over the passages he had encouraged them to read since the last time he had seen them. "People are coming in here every day, hungry to read and learn what God has for them," he said. "We're planning a big service Sunday morning, and that's just one day from now, so I'm going to be swamped." He explained much of what they had been reading, about what was to come once the Antichrist signed a pact with Israel.

"But do we even know when the Antichrist will come on the scene?" Lionel asked.

"No, but many of the scholars I've read seem to think he would have already been here by the time of the Rapture."

"Then it might be someone we already like and trust?" Vicki said. "I never followed politics much, but I heard people saying they thought President Fitzhugh was a liar, and—"

"I'd be very surprised if it was President Fitzhugh," Bruce said. "This week I want you to be reading the passages I have outlined on this sheet. It tells some of the characteristics of the Antichrist, and one of them is that he has some sort of blood ties with the Roman Empire."

"So he'll be an Italian?" Judd said.

"Not necessarily, but something in his ancestry will tie him to Rome. I don't believe that's true of our president, and after you have read these passages you may have other reasons why you agree with me that it's probably not him."

"Do you think he's here now?" Vicki asked. "Is there somebody you suspect?"

"I have my eye on an interesting world figure," Bruce said. "But it would be an awful mistake for me to try to identify the Antichrist before I was sure. Be watching and listening to the news. If the Antichrist is not a well-known world figure already, he probably soon will be. He's the one we're going to have to fight for at least seven years if we're going to survive until the Glorious Appearing."

"I want to survive," Lionel said. "But I remember my mother saying something about only a quarter of the people on earth after the Rapture still being alive at the end of the Tribulation."

"That's exactly what I believe the Bible teaches," Bruce said.

"Hold on a second," Judd said. "The population is already a lot less since the Rapture. Only one out of four of those will still be here when Jesus comes back again?"

"Because of the wars, plagues, famine, and disasters, yes," Bruce said. "I don't mean to scare you, but you don't have to be a rocket scientist to look around this room and see that there are four of us here."

"And you're saying," Vicki said, "that only

one of us is likely to be still alive in seven years?"

"Seven years from the signing of the treaty between Antichrist and Israel, yes."

Vicki's shoulders sagged, and she said just what Judd was thinking. "What's the use then? What are we here for?"

"That's the exciting part," Bruce said. "Our job is to win as many converts as possible before the end. Because when Jesus comes back to set up his thousand-year reign on earth, we'll either be here waiting for him or we'll come from heaven with him. Only those who come to him between the Rapture and the Millennium will reign with him."

"How many will that be?"

"Some of the scholars I'm studying estimate that the multitude of believers the book of Revelation calls 'numberless' could be as high as a billion and a half."

"I want to stay alive and see that," Vicki said.

Bruce smiled a tired smile. "I want to stay alive and be part of winning them," he said. "I'll talk more about it Sunday. You'll all be here, right?"

"Right," Judd said. "All of us. All four of us."

They heard a commotion outside: a squealing of bike tires, the dropping of a bike, the banging open of a door. Ryan rushed into the room, flushed, sweating, and—it appeared to Judd—just a little proud of himself. "Whew!" he said. "I made it!"

Judd, in spite of how relieved he was, couldn't help saying, "You're late."

"I know, but I called Bruce. You told them, didn't you, Bruce?" Bruce nodded. "I still get to stay in the house, right?"

Judd nodded. "Just tell us what happened."

Judd was amazed as Ryan told where he had been and what he was up to. At first Judd wasn't even sure he could believe the story, but it had a ring of truth to it. Lionel's mouth dropped open when Ryan told of the phone conversation he had overheard between Talia and André. Lionel looked like he wanted to leave right then and track down his uncle.

Ryan brought the story all the way up to where he was racing away on his bike, with Talia running after him and the van starting in the distance. "What did you do?" Vicki demanded. "Where did you go?"

He told them the whole story.

"Why didn't you call us?" Judd said when Ryan finished.

"I didn't have the number! The church's number is still on the notepad by our phone from the first time I wrote it down."

Judd was as excited as Ryan had been. He had reason to be pleased with himself. Maybe what he had done, getting so close to those people at Lionel's house, had not been smart. But he had stood up to them until he could escape, and his escape was perfect.

"You wanted that bad to stick with us, huh?" Judd said.

"You have no idea," Ryan said.

"And you'll be here Sunday with the rest of your friends?" Bruce said.

Ryan nodded. "This is where I'm supposed to be, I guess."

"What are you saying?"

"I got to thinking when I was on Raymie's street, what happens if LeRoy catches me? Or what happens if I don't see some car and shoot out in front of it? I could die. Then where would I be? I made my decision and said my prayer while I was on that bike. Is that OK? I mean, I didn't even have the breath to say it out loud. Does it still count?"

Bruce stood and embraced Ryan. "It sure does, buddy," he said. "God heard you. Welcome to the family."

Later Bruce helped load Ryan's bike into the trunk of Judd's car. "See you tomorrow," he said, and Judd noticed that as happy as Bruce had to be, he wasn't smiling. There was happiness once in a while, Judd realized, when something turned out the way they hoped. And he was sure everyone was as thrilled as he was that all four of them were now believers. But looking and acting happy was something totally different now from what it had been just a week before. There was too much to think about, too much to get used to, too much to overcome to be too smiley.

Ryan let out a big sigh, sitting next to Lionel in the backseat. "Wow," he said. "I don't ever want to have to go through that again. You can fight your own battles from now on, Lionel. I'm getting tired of looking out for you."

That almost made Judd smile. For now he was as exhausted as Ryan sounded. He was ready to sleep. And already he could hardly wait for Sunday morning.

FOUR

Sunday

JUDD was awakened early Sunday morning by a phone call from Bruce Barnes. "I'm concerned about Ryan," Bruce said, "and I'd like you to help me check up on him."

"He's still upset about his parents, of course," Judd said. "But he seemed a lot happier last night. Why are you worried about him?"

"Well, I have no doubt his decision was real," Bruce said. "I just want to make sure it wasn't something done totally out of fear. He was afraid something might happen to him, that Lionel's uncle's friends or enemies might catch him and kill him."

"Yeah?" Judd said. He wasn't following Bruce. "Does it make a difference? I mean, a big part of my reason was fear too."

"Yes, Judd," Bruce said, "but you also

understood, if I recall your story correctly, that you were a sinner and needed God's forgiveness."

"And you don't think Ryan thinks that?"

"I don't know. I'm just saying I didn't hear him say it. That doesn't mean his conversion didn't 'take,' but it's important to our faith and to our walk with Christ that we realize what he has saved us from. True guilt and sin have been washed away."

"You want me to ask him?"

"Not directly. I can probably do that better, being so much older than he is. I would have asked him last night, but I didn't have a chance to be alone with him, and I didn't want to embarrass him in front of you and the others."

Judd had to think about this. Maybe Ryan did have different reasons for finally making the decision he made, but not everyone came to Christ for the same reasons, did they? Of course, in the end they did. Everybody has the same problem—sin that keeps them from God. And it was by seeing and admitting that that Judd made his decision. But he also wanted to be with Christ and with his family when he died. And he wanted to avoid hell. Getting forgiven for being a sinner was a huge reason for him to do what he did, but the other stuff—being assured of heaven and staying out of hell—seemed almost as important. Did that mean his *own* decision had been based on fear? And was something wrong with that?

Bruce concluded by telling Judd that he was merely trying to be sure Ryan didn't think God was just some sort of a heavenly fire insurance salesman. Staying out of hell was one of the benefits of trusting him, but going from darkness to light, from death to life, from unforgiven sinner to sinner saved by grace, that was the crux of the decision.

On the way to the church that morning, Judd couldn't help prodding Ryan a little, just to see what he was thinking. Was he just the member of some new club with the only friends and "family" he had left? Or did he understand what had really happened to him? Maybe it was too much for someone his age to grasp. And yet, Judd reminded himself, when he was twelve, he knew the score. He simply had not acted on it and didn't really believe it was all that crucial. Needless to say, he did now.

"So, Ryan," Judd tried, "how does it feel to be part of the family?"

"Great," Ryan said. "I still miss my parents, and I know I always will. And I'm still hoping they somehow became Christians before they died. But I'm glad I'm going to heaven."

"Isn't it great to have our sins forgiven?" Judd said.

Vicki shot Judd a double take, which made him assume she sensed he was fishing for something. Lionel was not a morning person. He had leaned his head against the window in the backseat and seemed still to be sleeping.

"I guess," Ryan said. "I wasn't that much of a sinner, though."

"Oh, really?" Judd said. "You were the almost-perfect kid, huh?"

"No. But the only time I did bad stuff was when I was mad or something. I was never bad on purpose."

Now Vicki got into the discussion. "Never lied, never cheated, never stole, were never jealous of anybody or wanted revenge? Never gossiped?"

"Nothing that was really that bad," Ryan said. "Honest."

"But I'll bet you're glad that we don't get to heaven because of the good things we do."

"I don't know," Ryan said. "I might have made it. I was really a good kid."

"But you said yourself you weren't perfect, and only perfect people can get to God. And anyway, how can you say you might have made it? You *didn't* make it. Christ came and you were left behind, just like we were."

"I know," Ryan muttered, and he stopped talking. Judd was afraid he had scared Ryan off.

"I'm just saying," Judd said, "no matter how good or bad we are, no matter how much our good outweighs our bad, the whole point is that we fall short. We all need to be forgiven. That's what it means to be saved."

"So I'm not saved because I wasn't really a sinner? I mean, I guess I was a sinner the way everybody's a sinner, but because I didn't see myself that way?"

"How do you see yourself now?" Judd asked.

"Saved."

"From what?"

"Hell."

"But not from your sins?"

"Yeah, I guess."

"I'm telling you, man," Judd said. "We're all still sinners. But we're saved from our sins. Unless you're perfect—"

"I know I'm not perfect. But I was never that bad a guy."

"*I* was a bad person," Vicki said. "But my dad always said it was the people who don't see themselves as that bad who are the last ones to realize they need God."

"I knew I needed God because I didn't want to die and go to hell," Ryan said.

"And you would have gone to hell even as good a guy as you were, right?"

"'Course."

Judd thought Ryan was actually getting it. He would leave Ryan's training to Bruce. Judd knew he himself had much to learn. He and Lionel were the only two of these four who had been raised in church and had heard it all before. But now, with new eyes and new understanding, and—needless to say—a whole new life situation, he still felt like a baby when it came to the Bible and stuff about God. He could only assume Lionel felt the same way.

It was as if Judd couldn't get enough of what Bruce had to teach, and he couldn't wait to see what Bruce would talk about that morning. He had to park several blocks from the church, though they arrived several minutes before ten o'clock. The church was packed. Lots of people looked desperate and scared.

The four kids found the last seats together in the balcony. Chairs were set up on either side of the center aisle right next to the pews, and hundreds of people stood in the back.

Right at ten o'clock, Bruce began. The big pulpit on the platform was empty, and no lights shone up there. Bruce had placed a microphone stand in front of the first pew and spoke from there, holding his Bible and notes.

"Normally we at this church would be thrilled to see a crowd like this," he said. "But I'm not about to tell you how great it is to see you here. I know you're here seeking to know what happened to your children and loved ones, and I believe I have the answer. Obviously, I didn't have it before, or I too would be gone."

Bruce then told the same story he had told the kids, and his voice was the only sound in the place. Many wept as he spoke of his wife and children disappearing right from their beds. He showed the videotape the senior pastor had left, and more than a hundred people prayed along with the prayer at the end. Bruce urged them and anyone else who was interested to begin coming to New Hope.

He added, "I know many of you may still be skeptical. You may believe what happened was of God, but you still don't like it and you resent him for it. If you would like to come back and ask questions this evening, I will be here. Rest assured, we will be open to any honest question.

"I do want to open the floor to anyone who received Christ this morning and would like to confess it before us. The Bible tells us to do that, to make known our decision and our stand."

Judd leaned forward and peered down to the main part of the sanctuary, where the first to move was a tall, dark man, quickly followed to the microphone by dozens of others. "That's Raymie's dad!" Ryan whispered loudly.

The man introduced himself as Rayford Steele, an airline pilot, and Judd was captivated. As Rayford Steele told his story, of people disappearing off his plane over the Atlantic in the middle of the night on a flight to London, Judd's mouth dropped open. He had been on that very plane.

Most of the stories were the same as Captain Steele's. These people all seemed to have been on the edge of the truth because someone had warned them, but they had never fully accepted the truth about Christ.

Their stories were moving, and hardly anyone left, even when the clock swept past noon and forty or fifty more still stood in line. All seemed to need to tell of the ones who had been taken. Judd felt the same need, but he knew it would be a long, long time, even if he could get down to the main floor and get in line. Instead, he just listened.

At two o'clock, Judd's stomach was growling. Bruce finally interrupted, apologizing for having to bring the service to a close and teaching a simple chorus. Judd found himself overcome with emotion as he thought of the years when he had not enjoyed church at all. For how long had he ignored God, and how many times did he simply not sing when the congregation expressed its love for Christ? Now he sang through his tears, never meaning anything more in his life. And never did he miss his family as much as right then.

Judd and the other three returned that evening for the meeting of people who were still skeptical or had questions. Though he was no longer a skeptic, he sure had lots of questions. He was sure he would learn something. Many of the people were angry, wondering why God did things the way he did them. Bruce told them he wouldn't begin to try to explain God or speak for him, but that he was convinced God had given everyone ample opportunity to have been ready for the Rapture.

Others had question after question, and what Bruce couldn't answer from his education and recent reading, he promised to study and report back on later. Bruce concluded the long evening meeting by urging everyone present who had not made a decision for Christ to not put it off. "We never know what the next day, the next hour, the next moment may bring. I confess I never liked preachers saying that, trying to scare people into becoming believers by convincing them they were about to walk in front of a bus. But in this day and in this situation, people are dying all over the place. People you know. People you love. Captain Rayford Steele, who told his own story this morning, got some news from one of his flight attendants today that I have asked him to share this evening, just to illustrate this point."

When Captain Steele stepped to the microphone, he admitted that his story was about a man he did not even remember. "He was on my flight to London, the one during which so many passengers disappeared right out of their clothes. His name was Cameron Williams, and he was a writer for *Global Weekly* magazine."

Judd flinched. He remembered that guy. He had been the one who had helped the old man with his luggage in first class, and then had gone off looking for the man when his wife discovered only his clothes in the seat beside her. He was also the first one to jump down the evacuation chute when the plane had landed. He had flipped over forward and done a somersault, scraping the back of his head.

"I found out today that he eventually

made it to London, but that he was killed in a car bombing."

Judd shook his head. When would this end? People he knew and loved, people he had met or simply seen across the aisle on a plane—all dead. For whatever problems he had with his parents and his younger brother and sister, his life was tame compared to what the world had become. Who could keep up with it?

Captain Steele begged people to not wait. "You may have more questions," he said. "Ask them. Don't make a decision as important as this one without knowing for sure that you can believe with all your heart. But once your questions have been answered, don't risk your life and your afterlife by thinking you have all the time in the world. You don't."

The next day Vicki asked Judd to pick up a copy of *USA Today.* "I was sure never a news junkie before," she said. "But now I'm reading, watching, listening to everything. I want to know what's going on, who's who, and what's what. We have to be on the lookout for the Antichrist so we don't get fooled like so many people will."

Back at the house Vicki sat reading the paper while the television droned on. Every channel still carried news and emergency bulletins. No one complained that regular programming had not returned and likely wouldn't for a long time. The world was in chaos, and that was all anyone seemed to care about.

"Magazine Writer Assumed Dead," the *USA Today* headline read. "Cameron Williams, 30, the youngest senior writer of the staff of any weekly newsmagazine, is feared dead after a mysterious car bombing outside a London pub Saturday night that took the life of a Scotland Yard investigator."

"Judd!" Vicki called. "You'll want to see this."

Judd read the whole story over her shoulder. "Man, I can still hardly believe it. I sat right near that guy on the plane."

Ryan watched the news on television. Lionel was also in the room, but he was not watching. He was pacing, mumbling about finding his uncle André if it was the last thing he ever did. He ignored Judd and Vicki's talk about the dead writer. Judd noticed Lionel perk up, however, when the news shifted to the United Nations headquarters in New York.

"Even the press remains stunned this evening at the performance of Romanian President Nicolae Carpathia at the General Assembly of the United Nations," the news anchor said. "Just before Carpathia was scheduled to appear, the media was shocked to learn that Cameron 'Buck' Williams of *Global Weekly* was in attendance. Watch closely and you can see him, there, as the camera pans the press gallery. Williams had been thought dead in a car bombing in London last night. Investigation continues into his involvement in that scene, but as you can see, he is safe and sound now."

"What *is* this?" Judd said, his hand atop his head. "I can't keep up with everything! So now he's *not* dead?"

"Shh!" Vicki said. "Look at this guy!"

CNN was replaying the afternoon appearance at the UN of Nicolae Carpathia. He entered the assembly with a half dozen aides. He stood tall and dignified, yet he didn't seem cocky. He appeared an inch or two over six feet tall, broad shouldered, thick chested, trim, athletic, tanned, and blond. His shock of hair was trimmed neatly around the ears, sideburns, and neck, and he wore a navy blue business suit with a matching tie.

Even on television, the man seemed to carry himself with a sense of humility and purpose. He dominated the room, and yet he did not seem impressed with himself. His jaw and nose were broad and prominent, and his blue eyes were set deep under thick brows.

First to speak was UN Secretary-General Mwangati Ngumo of Botswana. He announced that the assemblage was privileged to hear from the new president of Romania and that an Israeli dignitary would formally introduce him. A little old man with a heavy accent introduced Carpathia as "a young man I respect and admire as much as anyone I've ever met."

With courtly manners, Carpathia remained at the side of the lectern until the older man was seated, then stood relaxed and smiling before speaking without notes. Judd was astounded to notice that he never hesitated, misspoke, or took his eyes off his audience.

Judd was impressed that Carpathia spoke earnestly and with passion. He mentioned that he was aware that it had not been a full week yet since the disappearance of millions all over the world, including many who would have been "in this very room." Carpathia spoke in perfect English with only a hint of a Romanian accent. Occasionally he used one of the nine languages in which he was fluent, each time translating himself into English. He was articulate, carefully enunciating every syllable.

Judd realized how strange it was that he

was watching news like this. He would have cared nothing for this kind of thing a week before. Now he was fascinated. Here was a man with confidence and maybe some answers. He sure seemed like a great guy.

Carpathia began by announcing that he was humbled and moved to visit "for the first time this historic site, where nation after nation has set its sights. One by one they have come from all over the globe on pilgrimages as sacred as any to the Holy Lands, exposing their faces to the heat of the rising sun. Here they have taken their stand for peace in a once-and-for-all, rock-solid commitment to putting behind them the insanity of war and bloodshed. These nations, great and small, have had their fill of the death and maiming of their most promising citizens in the prime of their youth.

"From lands distant and near they have come: from Afghanistan, Albania, Algeria. . . ." He continued, his voice rising and falling dramatically with the careful pronunciation of the name of each member country of the United Nations. Judd heard a passion in his voice, a love for these countries and the ideals of the UN. Carpathia was clearly moved as he plunged on, listing country by country in alphabetical order by memory.

Judd noticed the other three kids were as riveted by this as he was. At the UN, people began standing and clapping with the mention of each new country name. More than five minutes into the recitation, Carpathia had not missed a beat. He had never once hesitated, stammered, or mispronounced a syllable. When he got to the *U*'s and came to "The United States of America," Judd applauded, Vicki smacked her hands together once, Lionel raised a fist, and Ryan said, "Yes!"

By the end of his list of nearly two hundred nations, Nicolae Carpathia was at an emotional, fevered pitch. Delegates and even the press stood and cheered. The tape ended and TV viewers were switched back to CNN news where the anchorman sat shaking his head in amazement. "Talk about a man taking a city by storm," he said. "They're already calling him Saint Nick, and he's the toast of New York."

"The Antichrist, whoever he is, will have to face this guy sometime," Vicki said. "I'd like to see that."

"Me too," Judd said. "Wonder how he missed the Rapture. He sure seems like a Christian."

"I never cared about politics before," Lionel said. "But this man is something else.

Just hearing him makes me want to find my uncle, and right now."

"I'll help," Ryan said.

"We all will," Judd said.

FIVE

Finding André

LIONEL Washington didn't really want everyone else's help, and he told them that. "Talia is André's old fiancée. I didn't know they were back together, but if they are, maybe she'll tell me something."

"You don't want us to go with you?" Judd asked. "I could drive you."

"I'm going to ride my bike. You guys don't need to get in trouble with these people."

"Why don't you go during the day?" Vicki said.

"Yeah," Judd said. "It's dark. How do we know when to come looking for you?"

"I'll be fine."

"Don't even say that," Vicki said. "You heard what almost happened to Ryan."

"If we don't hear from you by eleven," Judd said, "we'll come after you."

"I have no idea where I'll be. André's not going to be at my house."

"What are we supposed to do if we don't hear from you?"

"I'll be fine, all right?"

"No," Judd said. "We agreed to look out for each other. We're going to have to follow you, that's all."

"I don't like this," Lionel said.

"You won't even see us," Judd said. "We'll worry about you, but you won't have to worry about us. Now get going."

Lionel jogged out to his bike and rode directly home. Judd had been right. Lionel was not aware of Judd following him. He was still certain he would be safe, but it did make him feel better to know that the others cared about him.

Lights were on, but no cars were in the driveway. Who was there? Lionel stepped to the door and raised his hand to knock, suddenly realizing how silly that was. *This is my own house,* he thought. He walked in and went straight upstairs to his room. He heard quick footsteps from a back room downstairs. They came across the hardwood floors in the living room, into the dining room, and up the stairs.

"LeRoy?" Talia called out. "I didn't see you guys pull in."

Lionel stepped into the hall and could tell he had startled her. "Hey, Talia," he said simply. "I need you to take me to André."

"Yeah, right," she said. "Like I know where he is."

"I know you know where he is," Lionel said. "And if you don't take me to him, he's going to be upset."

"I heard he was dead," she said.

"Cut the baloney," Lionel said. "We both know you chased off a friend of mine today. He heard you talking to André on the phone, and it was obvious he was worried about me."

"If I hear from him," she said, "I'll tell him you're fine."

"Is there a car in the garage?"

She hesitated. "No. There's not. Why?"

Lionel sensed she was lying. "I know there is," he said. "C'mon and take me."

"That's LeRoy's two-seat roadster. He'll kill me if I take it."

"You're not takin' it," Lionel said. "You're borrowing it. You'll probably be back before LeRoy is."

Talia appeared to be thinking it over. "I wouldn't mind seein' André myself," she said. "LeRoy and them haven't been getting back before one or two in the morning the last coupla nights anyway."

"Let's go," Lionel said.

"I'd better call him first."

"Who? LeRoy?"

"No! André!"

"We both know he's hiding out. He's not going anywhere."

"You think of everything, you little brat. And there's no way you're only thirteen."

Lionel ignored her, taking both comments as compliments.

The roadster was a cool car, Lionel thought, and had it not been for the disappearances of his family and the danger in which he now found himself, he might have been impressed enough to really check it out. He had been interested in unusual cars since he was a small child. But now this was just a way to get to André. Something to ride in.

Talia seemed unable to concentrate even on where she was going. All she could say, over and over, was "Ooh, LeRoy's gonna kill me if he finds out about this!"

Lionel tried to talk to her, mostly to simply change the subject. "So, Talia," he said, "where were you when the disappearances happened?"

"What?" she said, as if demanding to know what in the world he was talking about. "Where *was* I?"

"Yeah. Simple question. Everybody

remembers where they were. I was sleeping in my basement with André. Where were you?"

"I was at a party André shoulda been at. So he was with you?"

"He didn't tell you where he was?"

"No! I told you! He's usually at all the parties, but he owed these guys some money, so I figured he was laying low."

"I thought he was hanging with us because we're family."

"Oh, yeah," Talia said. "That's André. Big family man."

"He could be, at times."

"I know. Whenever he really needed something, he played you guys like banjos. When he needed cash or a place to crash, he'd run back to the family and get religion. Am I right? Huh? Am I right?"

Lionel shook his head and looked out the window. Talia was driving toward Chicago. It didn't seem to slip past her that Lionel had ignored her question. "Tell me," she said. "Isn't that what André pulled on your family every time?"

Lionel nodded, but she must not have seen him. "Isn't it?" she pressed.

"Yeah," Lionel muttered. "So, what did you think when people disappeared?"

"Nobody disappeared from *that* party,

honey. Made me start believin' it was only Jesus' people who flew away."

"You believe that?"

"No! I'm just sayin' . . ."

"That's what I believe, Talia."

She whirled to face him. "No lie?"

"No lie," Lionel assured her, nodding toward the road where another car was signaling to move into Talia's lane. Lionel hated when she took her eyes from the road. She was an erratic enough driver when she was paying attention.

"So," she said, "how'd you miss out then, comin' from a family like yours? André says they're all gone but him and you."

"Right," Lionel said, and for the next several minutes and most of the ride to Chicago, he told her his story.

Lionel almost wished he hadn't started on the subject. Within minutes, Talia was wiping her eyes with her fingers while still trying to maneuver LeRoy's roadster through Chicago traffic. Lionel was eager to reconnect with André, but he didn't want Talia crying and driving at the same time. He was relieved when she finally pulled to the side of a street about six blocks south of where the police found the body they thought was André's.

Talia shifted into park and buried her face in her hands. "My mama's gone too," she wailed. "I knew the truth. I always knew the truth. I was raised the same way you were. Well, maybe not the same, but Mama warned me and warned me about this!"

"It's not too late, Talia," Lionel said. "I'm a believer now, and so are three of my friends and lots of other people—"

"No! No! It's too late. When Jesus took the Christians away, the Holy Ghost left and nobody can be saved anymore!"

"That's not in the Bible," Lionel said. "You need to talk to our pastor."

"Your pastor was left behind?" Talia said.

Lionel told Bruce's story. "And he told us the Bible talks about a great harvest of souls during the last seven years of the world. Something like a billion and a half people will get saved, and there'll be like 144,000 Jewish evangelists."

"Even if what you're saying is true, Lionel," Talia said, "I know I'm too far gone. If there really is a second chance, I don't deserve one, I know that."

"Nobody deserves a *first* chance. If we had to deserve it, nobody would make it."

To Lionel it appeared that Talia suddenly realized she was pouring her heart out to a thirteen-year-old boy. She quickly wiped her eyes again, turned the rearview mirror so she could check her face, and quit crying. "André is close by," she said, "but I'm gonna have to let him know you're here and find out if he wants to see you."

"Never mind," Lionel said, reaching for his door handle. "He does."

"You can't just barge in there with me," she said.

"Yes, I can, and you know it. You know he wants to see me."

Talia hesitated. She snorted. "True enough," she said. "He probably wants to see you more than he wants to see me."

Lionel got out of the car, prepared to follow Talia. As he fell into step behind her, he said, "You two not getting along?"

"I'd still marry him, messed up as he is."

"He doesn't want to?"

"Obviously! But I'm scared to death to be facin' the future alone."

"But André is *really* messed up," Lionel said.

"Not as much as me," she said.

Lionel wondered what kind of a couple those two would make.

Talia led Lionel around the back of a three-story brick apartment building in a bad neighborhood. Lionel wondered if Judd and the others were still keeping track of him. In a way he hoped they were, but he also wondered what three white kids would do to protect him in *this* neighborhood.

As they approached the rear entrance, Lionel noticed the lights went off in the apartment at that end on the top floor. As they climbed the square staircase, Lionel was quickly enveloped in odors and noise. People were apparently cooking, arguing, and fighting.

As they reached the third floor, where the lights at the end of the building had gone out, Talia put a finger to her lips and knocked four times at the door. Silence.

She knocked four times again. "Open up, André!" she called out. "It's jes' me."

"Somebody's with you!" André hissed from just inside the door. "Who is that?"

"It's your nephew! Now open up!"

Before the words were out of her mouth, André had begun the process of unlocking, unbolting, unchaining, and opening the door. He peered out from the dark apartment, then grabbed Talia and Lionel and yanked them inside. He shut, locked, bolted, and chained the door in the dark. "Now," he said finally. "Let's get a look at you."

Lionel couldn't help but chuckle. His uncle had always been a little crazy, but—

"It'll be a long time before my eyes get used to the darkness and I can see you," Lionel said. "Get a light on in here."

Lionel heard André feeling along the wall

for a switch. When a single, bare bulb came on above them, Lionel was stunned to see his wasted uncle. André was barefoot and wore a pair of old, shiny suit pants and a sleeveless T-shirt with food stains down the front. He appeared to not have bathed for days. His hair was matted, his facial hair patchy. His breath smelled of alcohol, and his dark eyes were bloodshot. It was all Lionel could do to keep from gasping and telling his uncle how bad he looked. Lionel assumed André knew that and didn't care.

"Oh, André!" was all Talia seemed to be able to say, and when he approached her, she stiffened. Whatever relationship was there or had been there or was trying to be rekindled, Lionel knew André's present condition wasn't helping.

"Ain't there no shower in this place?" she finally managed.

André shrugged. "Yeah, I guess."

"Get your stinking self in there and get cleaned up," she said. "Shave and brush your teeth too, and don't be comin' back out here until you do."

André squinted at her and looked as if he were about to burst into tears, but his shoulders sagged and he skulked away like a little boy who'd been ordered about by his mother. "Oh, man!" he whined.

"Hey," Lionel said. "I haven't got all night. I got people who worry about me when I get in late."

"That's more than I can say," Talia said, collapsing into a plastic chair at the Formica-topped dinette table. A heavy, glass ashtray full of butts and a nearly empty bottle of cheap wine graced the table. Talia noticed them as if an ugly insect had just landed before her.

"Oh, for the love of all things . . . ," she said, never finishing the thought. She had just used her foot to slide out another chair for Lionel when she stood and grabbed the wine bottle in one hand and the ashtray in the other. She tossed the bottle into a waste-basket nearly full of beer cans, where it settled at a crazy angle. She held the ashtray at eye level, looked resolutely at Lionel, and let it drop. It smashed the wine bottle, and Lionel heard the last of the wine drip to the bottom of the basket. The contents of the ashtray, however, scattered on the floor. Talia swore.

Steam poured from under the door of the nearby bathroom. Over the sound of the cascading water, André hollered, "What's goin' on out there?"

"I'm just clearin' the table," Talia

answered. "What you been doin' for food, just drinkin'?"

"That's all the food I need!" André said. "Don't be messin' with my hooch."

Lionel was disgusted. He was relieved to know that André was still alive, if you could call this living. There was always a chance for André if he didn't kill himself or get himself killed first.

Was this the life André thought was better than what the rest of the family enjoyed? There had never been cigarettes or booze in Lionel's house. When guests asked his mother if she minded if they smoked, she always said kindly, "Of course not. I have an air-conditioned facility for you just beyond that door." It was the door to the driveway. And when Mrs. Washington's colleagues at *Global Weekly* magazine forgot themselves and showed up at dinner parties with gifts of expensive liquor or wine, or if they sent the same as Christmas gifts, she thanked them politely. She did not serve the stuff, of course, but the next day sold it to the manager of the beverage department at the corner store and gave the entire amount to the church. "The devil used that money long enough," she would tell her husband sweetly, winking at Lionel. "It's time the Lord got it back."

How Lionel missed his mama at times like

this! What had he been thinking when he considered being a rebel with André better than being part of the family of God?

The only things André had to change into were brightly colored and way-too-big workout shorts and a T-shirt that had been left in the apartment. Lionel could only wonder whose place this was and whose clothes those were. André padded out, keeping the shorts up with one hand.

"You look better," Talia said, smiling. "But not much."

André did not smile. "Man," he said, "it's good to see you both."

Lionel was frustrated. This was no family reunion. This was the only family he had left. "André," Lionel said, "I want to know what happened after you left that crazy message on my answering machine."

But the phone rang. André jumped, then stared at Talia. "How'd you get here?" he asked.

"I borrowed LeRoy's roadster."

"What? He doesn't loan that out!"

"He doesn't exactly know."

"Oh, man!"

André answered the phone and immediately glared at Talia. "LeRoy!" he mouthed silently. "And he's not happy."

SIX

Answers

André stood and paced, stretching the phone cord to its limit. He whined, cried, begged, explained, and tried to cover for Talia. "It was my fault, man," he told LeRoy. "I called and begged her to come here and see me. . . . Anyone with her? No, why do you ask? . . . No, you don't need to come here! She'll be right back. . . . I just needed to see her, that's all. I want to get out of here! When can I live with you guys? . . . I did my part! . . . I'm not telling you what to do. I'm just askin'."

Lionel had no idea what LeRoy was saying, but André was as scared as Lionel had ever seen him. "I'll send her right home, LeRoy," André said, "but remember, this was all my idea. Don't take it out on her."

André hung up. "LeRoy's mad," he said.

"No kidding," Talia said. "And you were a

lying wuss. Don't you ever get tired of being a coward?"

"I was just trying to protect you, girl. You ought to be grateful."

"You were protectin' yourself, André! And I don't need your help."

"LeRoy will kill you and never think twice about it. You'd better get back there."

"We're going," she said. Come on, Lionel."

"I'm not going anywhere," Lionel said. "I need some answers, and I'll find my own way back."

"Yeah, right," Talia said. "Let's go."

"I'm not going," Lionel insisted. "Go if you want to."

"Well, I've got to go. If you want to find your own way back—"

"If you don't get back soon, Talia," André said, "LeRoy will come looking for you, and we don't want that."

"This bus is pullin' out, Lionel," Talia said. "Last call, all aboard."

He waved her off.

"Suit yourself," she said, as if he had made the dumbest decision ever. She went through the whole unlocking routine to let herself out, and then André had to lock up again.

"What is all this about?" Lionel demanded. "Talk to me!"

But André had turned out the lights and crept to the window to keep track of Talia on her way to the car. "Ooh, that *is* LeRoy's roadster! Oh, man!"

"What'd you think, we were lying? Now, c'mon, André! I've been worried about you for days!"

"Shh!" André said, still peering out the window. "You don't know what kind of trouble I'm in, and if you're not out of here soon, you're gonna be right in it with me."

Lionel turned the light on, and André ducked away from the window, crashing into a chair. "Don't do that!" he said. "Somebody'll see me!"

"Who are you afraid of? LeRoy isn't even around here."

"How do you know? He wasn't at your house, or he never would have let Talia leave with you."

"Is he coming here?"

"He might. Not too many other people know where I am."

"What's it all about, André? You make that crazy call and leave a long message on our machine that sounds like you're going to kill yourself, and when I get to your place to check on you, the cops tell me you committed suicide and where I can identify the body. So I go to the place and there you are, but it's not you. Who killed himself or got himself murdered wearing your clothes and carrying your identification?"

André sat and buried his head in his hands. "I didn't mean it to come to all this," he wailed. He was interrupted yet again, this time by another knock on the door. He looked up with a start and motioned frantically for Lionel to turn off the light. Lionel did, but then turned it back on when he heard Talia's voice.

"It's just me," she whispered loudly through the door. "Don't open up. I just wanted to tell you there's an expensive car full of white kids down the block. Looks like they're up to no good, but they're in the wrong neighborhood. They're going to get that nice car stole. If you pulled that off, André, you might be back in good with LeRoy."

"I ought to already be back in good with LeRoy," André said, but Lionel was beginning to unlock the door.

"Don't be openin' up now," Talia insisted. "I'm going."

"No!" Lionel said. "Wait!" He got the door open. "Those are my friends down there. Tell 'em I'm all right and that they should wait for me. They're my ride home."

Talia rolled her eyes and shrugged. "Whatever. But that car would sure get LeRoy's attention."

"You and LeRoy already hassled one of the kids in that car," Lionel said. "One more deal like that and you'll be out of my house sooner than you think."

"Ooh, tough guy," she said. "I'll tell your chauffeur you're on your way."

André and Lionel fell silent, listening to Talia's footsteps all the way down the stairs and out into the alley, where she fired up the roadster. Lionel turned out the light, and they watched out the window as she pulled down the street and stopped next to Judd's car. Lionel only hoped the others would believe her and not come charging in to rescue him. Who knew what Ryan would do after having been chased by her and LeRoy earlier?

Lionel was mad. "Turn the light on, Uncle André," he said. The word *uncle* nearly stuck in his throat because he sure had seen a new and unattractive side of André. He didn't seem older or wiser or worthy of any respect like he sometimes used to. Now it seemed as if Lionel was the one who should be in charge. Maybe André was in trouble, but did that justify his acting like such a wimp? What was wrong with him?

They both knew that the faith they had

turned their backs on before was right and true and could save them now, so why was it only Lionel, the younger of them, who had seen the light?

André turned the light on and sat down, as if expecting a lecture. But a lecture was not what Lionel had in mind. He had a lot of questions, and he wanted answers.

"When you called my house, drinking and crying and slobbering and talking about killing yourself, were you serious or were you put up to that?"

"Both."

"What do you mean? Part of that was just acting?"

"Part of it," André said, staring at the floor.

"I was worried to death about you. I didn't want you to go to hell. Anyway, we're family, man. We're all we've got left. We've got to watch out for each other."

"Listen, Lionel, I'm going to hell whether you want me to or not."

"You want to?"

"'Course not! But that's where people like me go!"

"I'm not going there!" Lionel said. "And I used to be like you."

"You were just a kid. I was afraid I was the one who made you what you were. I'm so glad you're a Christian now."

"Then why aren't you?"

"It's too late for me."

"You know better than that! You know the truth. You just have to act on it now, André."

"You have no idea."

"Then tell me! What's going on? I want to know!"

André stood, paced, then sat again. He let out a huge sigh. "All right," he said finally. "That guy found in my apartment was one of the guys I owed money to."

"Really? He wasn't one of the two I met that one time, was he? He sure didn't look like them. They were both a lot bigger."

"Those two just worked for him. They were his collection guys. When they couldn't get any money out of me, he came lookin' for me. It was pay up or be killed. I had held out on him way too long. Well, I had no money, and LeRoy wasn't about to advance me any, so it came down to kill or be killed. That's when I called you. I didn't want to die. If I was going to go, I was going to go on my own terms. I'd rather kill myself than die that way."

"So you were serious."

"Well, mostly. LeRoy had come up with a plan. He knew this guy I owed the money to, see, and he was the one who reminded me that the guy was my size. It was LeRoy's idea to get him to come to my place for the money. He told me to leave some message somewhere that would make it look like I killed myself. I called your machine, left that message, talked about how guilty I felt about you and all that, and then even wrote a suicide note.

"After the guy showed up, LeRoy's friends had his people outnumbered and ran them off. While the guy thinks he's got his bodyguards protecting him from the hallway, LeRoy pops out of the closet and gets the drop on the guy. He makes him put on my clothes and put my wallet and stuff in his pocket. He put on my rings and watch and everything. Then LeRoy told me to off him."

"Kill him?"

"Yeah. But I couldn't do it. I had the blade and everything to make it look like a suicide. I was afraid the guy would fight and make it look obvious that someone had done it to him, but LeRoy had thought of that too. He tells the guy he's going to die anyway and gets the guy crying and begging and starts loading him up with whiskey. This is real strong stuff now, the good stuff, not like I'm used to drinking. He gets the guy so mellow and out of it that he didn't even struggle. I was supposed to cut him, but I couldn't even do that."

"Of course you couldn't kill someone, André. You know better than that."

"Oh, don't be makin' me out as some kind of saint now, Lionel. Fact is, I wish I could have done it. LeRoy was setting me up, don't you see? I had told him all about your house and how I knew you would let us stay there and everything. But once he set up this fake suicide and murdered the guy, he made sure he had something on me."

"What does he have on you? You owe him money too?"

"No! Think, boy! We never expected you to go identify the body. We figured you'd get the word and believe it was me, and that would be the end of it. But now that you told the cops it wasn't me, it won't be long before they figure out who the victim was, and guess who looks guilty? I mean, the guy was found in my place in my clothes. If it's not me, it has to be someone I murdered and made to look like me, right?"

Lionel nodded slowly. "So, you're hiding out from everybody. The dead guy's men. The cops. Anybody who might know you and spread the word you're alive."

"Exactly."

"André, I never told the cops it wasn't your body I saw."

André stood quickly. "What? You didn't? Are you sure?"

"'Course I'm sure. I was spooked by that place, and I was so shocked it wasn't you that I just left."

"You didn't even tell the coroner?"

"The only people who know are my friends and my pastor."

André clapped and danced. "Oh, man!" he shouted. "I love you!"

Lionel sat and put both hands atop his head. "I don't know what you're so happy about. No matter how you look at it, you were there when a guy was murdered. You're in on it. You're as guilty as LeRoy."

"Technically, legally, yeah, I guess," André said, and the full realization hit Lionel how far gone his uncle truly was. "But don't you see? LeRoy's really got nothing hanging over my head! I can go live in your house with those guys. My debt is gone because the guy I owed is dead. LeRoy can't keep me hidden away because there's no need. I can just use a new name, get new papers, and nobody's the wiser."

Lionel suddenly felt very old. André was more than twice his age, and as usual, André seemed to know less than he did. How long could he get by after coming out of hiding before someone who knew him put the word out that he wasn't dead after all? Sure, the cops had a lot of other stuff to do with all the chaos that had come from the disappearances. But no one was going to look the other way when there had been an obvious murder. An apparent suicide victim is in the morgue, and yet people see him on the streets? Lionel was amazed at the shortsightedness, the stupidity of his uncle. More, though, he was heartbroken at André's complete lack of guilt or sense of responsibility for what had happened. Maybe the guy who died was a bad guy who deserved it. He had probably killed people himself. But that didn't make his death any less of a murder, and André, was in it up to his ears.

Lionel stood and moved to the door. "Tell LeRoy what you told me," André said. "I mean, I'll call him, but he won't believe me unless you tell him too. Then I'll be back at your house before you know it."

Lionel just shook his head as he began the unlocking routine again. "Uncle André," he said, turning to face him, "you have only one chance. You have to tell what you know about the murder, admit you were part of it."

André laughed. "Yeah, good plan. I don't go to heaven when Jesus comes back, I have to live through the Tribulation, I'm on my way to hell, and you want me to spend what's left of my miserable life in prison."

"What I want is for you to do what's right."

"I've never done what's right," André said. And for the first time that evening, Lionel thought André was right on the money.

SEVEN

Getting Closer

IT WAS getting late. Judd was tired and knew the others had to be too. He had sat in that idling car for more than an hour, including when the young black woman showed up alone and told Judd that Lionel would be down soon.

"Is he all right?" Judd asked her as Ryan slid off the backseat and crouched on the floor.

"Yeah," Talia said. "He's all right as long as he's with his uncle. André ain't gonna do nothin' to his own blood. And you can tell your little spy in the back there that he can come out of hiding. Next time LeRoy sees him on our property, though, he's going to be in deep dirt."

Vicki laughed.

Talia leaned in past Judd, who backed up

to make room. "What's your problem, little wench?"

"I'm not the one with the problem," Vicki said, and Judd was stunned at her casual tone. She must have had a lot of experience talking tough to older people. "You're the one referring to Lionel's house as your property. What a joke."

"You don't see me laughin'," Talia said.

"How long do you guys think you can get away with just moving into a person's house without his permission?"

"Long as you mind your own business," Talia said. "I wouldn't be messin' with stuff that's none of your concern."

"As long as Lionel's our friend, his trouble *is* our business."

Talia had waved them off and hurried back to her car. That's when Judd began to worry. He kept an eye on the clock, and time seemed to drag.

"Is she gone?" Ryan asked from the floor of the backseat.

"Yes," Vicki said, turning to talk to him. "You don't have to be afraid of her."

"You didn't see this LeRoy guy. He looks like he could whip anybody. I'm afraid of all of 'em."

"Not me," Vicki said.

"That was obvious," Judd said. "Why not?"

"It wasn't that long ago I was a brat and didn't care what I said to adults. They hardly ever follow through on their threats, and what are they going to do anyway? I mean, these people may be the real thing, but they aren't going to waste their time hassling kids like us."

"Except they have to worry that Lionel is eventually going to go to the police."

"That's why they keep trying to intimidate him. That stuff doesn't work on me. I don't want to be mean, but she didn't scare me at all."

"You'd be scared if LeRoy was chasin' you," Ryan said.

"That is probably true," Vicki said.

Judd grew tenser as the night wore on. "We said we were going to come looking for Lionel if we didn't hear from him by eleven," he said.

"But we heard from him through the woman," Vicki said.

"She could have been lying. Why should we trust her?"

"That message had to come from Lionel. Otherwise, how would she know we were his friends?"

"You have to admit, Vick, we look a little out of place here."

Vicki shot Judd a double take. "Why did you call me 'Vick'?"

Judd shrugged. "Just a nickname. Sorry."

"I don't mind," she said. "It's just that my big brother always called me that. I miss him so much." She turned away and covered her eyes with her hand.

"Sorry," Judd said again.

"It's all right," she managed. "I like remembering him."

"I'm really tired," Ryan said. "If this wasn't such a scary place, I'd be sleeping right now."

"I wouldn't be able to sleep here either, partner," Judd said.

"Oh, man!" Ryan said, falling to the floor again. "That van that just turned into the alley! That's got to be LeRoy!"

"Are you sure?"

"How could I forget that ugly thing chasing me all through the neighborhood?"

"Oh, great," Judd said, glancing at Vicki, who quickly wiped her eyes and turned to look around the area.

"We've got to get Lionel out of there," she said, reaching for the door handle. "Let's go."

"Just a minute," Judd said. "We don't know what we're walking into. What if LeRoy's armed, or not alone? And where exactly *is* Lionel? And is there more than one way out of that alley?"

"Let's just go home," Ryan whined.

A figure appeared in the rearview mirror. Judd whispered, "Uh-oh," and put the car in gear. When the figure reached for the back door, Judd floored the accelerator, and the car screeched away from the curb.

The figure slapped the car and shouted, "Hey!"

"Oh, no!" Ryan shouted. "Go! Go!"

Judd was going all right, until Vicki whirled around and stared behind them. "That's Lionel!" she said. "Go back! Go back!"

Judd slid to a stop and threw the car into reverse. He wasn't used to speeding backwards and twice veered into the curb. That must have made Lionel wonder about his safety because Judd saw him skip up onto the sidewalk. When Judd finally stopped near Lionel, he was stunned to see Lionel chuckling.

"What did I do, scare you guys?" he said, as he slid into the backseat. "And what're you doin' on the floor, Ryan?"

Judd floored the gas pedal again, but he had forgotten to shift into drive, and the car jumped back and over the curb, narrowly missing a light pole and stopping inches from a brick wall. "Hey! Whoa!" Lionel said, laughing. "You're safe in this neighborhood, now that you've got a brother in the car."

Judd was relieved he had not hit Lionel or the wall but was also embarrassed at being such a klutz. He was soon speeding away, only to have to stop quickly at a red light a few blocks away. "Didn't you see LeRoy?" Judd demanded.

"LeRoy? No, Talia brought me to see André. They've got him holed up in—"

"I mean didn't you just see LeRoy pull into that alley?"

Lionel turned around in his seat. "Are you sure?"

"We're sure," Ryan muttered from the floor.

"Get up here, will you?" Lionel said. "You're safe now."

Ryan clambered into the seat. "He was drivin' that ugly old brown and yellow van," he said.

"Must've been him all right," Lionel said. "We'd better go back."

"Right," Judd said sarcastically. "I'm gonna go back there and face LeRoy in the middle of the night."

"Yes," Vicki said. "Let's."

"No!" Ryan wailed. "I've been brave enough for one day."

"Yeah," Lionel said. "You're brave as long as you can camp out on the floor out of sight."

Judd didn't know what to do. He felt responsible for Lionel, but was André his problem too? He pulled to the side of the street after getting a green light.

"We're not going back, are we?" Ryan said.

"Just let me think," Judd said.

"We have to," Vicki said.

"If you don't go back, I'm going to have to go on my own," Lionel said. "He's my uncle, and I have to make sure LeRoy doesn't do something stupid. Once LeRoy figures out that I'm onto him and that my friends know, André is as good as dead."

"Well," Judd said, "I can't let you go back alone, but I don't think we all need to go either."

"I don't want to go at all," Ryan said.

"We got that message," Lionel said.

"I don't want to get this car down in there and not be able to get out," Judd said.

"C'mon," Vicki said, "let's just walk back with Lionel and see what we can see."

"You can't leave the car here either," Lionel said. "You'll come back to a pile of trash or maybe to a pile of nothing."

Judd sighed. He felt responsible for everyone. It wasn't fair to make Ryan face LeRoy again. And how could Judd ensure his safety? He breathed a silent prayer. He didn't know how to tell yet when God was leading him directly. He decided to use his best judgment and assume that was from God.

"Vicki," he said, "Lionel and I will go back and be sure André's all right. You and Ryan stay here with the car—"

"Oh, I wanted to go," Vicki said. "I'm not afraid of—"

"Just do this for me," Judd said. "I don't have time to argue about it, but I'm not leaving the car here or Ryan here alone."

"Thank you!" Ryan shouted.

Vicki shook her head. "OK," she muttered.

"I hate to leave you out of it," Judd said. "But I don't know what else—"

"Just go," she said. "I understand."

It didn't seem like she understood or agreed, but Judd didn't have the time to persuade her. He took her word for the fact that she was all right with his decision, and he and Lionel headed back. "Keep the doors locked and the engine running," Lionel said as they left. "And don't talk to anyone but a cop."

It appeared to Judd that he and Lionel were the only ones on the street at that time of the night. He followed Lionel, who loped down the sidewalk and cut in to the first alley he could find. Half a block in that direction he took a right and was headed directly back to where he had visited André. He pointed and said, "Three blocks up. That three-story building."

The words were barely out of Lionel's mouth when Judd heard what sounded like a firecracker. Lionel stopped and Judd ran into him, knocking him flat on his face. Lionel sat up and groaned as Judd apologized. Lionel pulled up his jeans to display scrapes on both knees. His hands and elbows were scraped raw too.

"I'm sorry, man," Judd said over and over. "I heard that pop, but I didn't see you stop."

"I'm all right," Lionel said through clenched teeth. "Let's keep going." But as he stood, a huge shock wave and then a deafening explosion rocked the alleyway. It knocked Lionel back onto his seat and made Judd cover his ringing ears.

"Oh no, oh no!" Lionel said, scrambling to his feet and running toward André's building. As they closed the gap, Judd saw flames leaping from the top-story window. Within seconds, flames engulfed the third floor. Judd stared at the fire as he ran and was startled when Lionel slowed and turned around, catching him and flinging him up against a building in the alley.

"What—?" he began, then noticed headlights coming fast and furious. He and Lionel plastered themselves back against the wall as the careening vehicle bore down on them. The alley was barely wide enough for them and the truck, or whatever it was. As it scraped the wall across from them on its way by, Judd saw it was a brown and yellow van. Crazily, he noticed the vertical row of decals running down the passenger side of the front windshield.

"That's got to be LeRoy!" Lionel shouted, and ran on. Judd stood staring at the back of the van as it darted from side to side and scraped buildings, hit garbage cans, and nearly rolled over as it shot left out of the alley and onto the street. He worried that LeRoy would see Vicki and Ryan in his car as he raced by.

When Judd turned back, Lionel was long gone. Judd raced toward the burning building, making out Lionel's silhouette ahead of him as he ran. He hoped against hope Lionel wouldn't try to get into that place, but he knew he would do the same if *his* last living relative were trapped in there.

Lionel didn't hesitate. He blasted through the door on the first floor as other people were making their way out, screaming and hollering. The entire third floor was enveloped in fire, and Judd saw a burly man in just his undershorts and T-shirt trying to keep Lionel from getting all the way in.

Lionel quickly evaded him, and soon Judd was near the entrance himself and faced a decision.

Everything in him wanted to run the other way. He knew it wouldn't be long before the fire began dropping embers to the other floors. This building would not be saved. Dozens of tenants hurried from the place, gathering in clusters as far as they could get from the fire.

Judd stood on the walkway leading to the back door, squinting against the orange light of the flames and holding an arm before his face to shield his cheeks from the searing heat. He could hardly believe a fire still thirty feet above him could radiate like that. Judd reached the door and peeked around the people who streamed out. He caught sight of Lionel bobbing and weaving and darting up the stairs between, around, and sometimes over the escapees. Some tried to restrain him, but he fought them off, clearly not willing to be held back.

Surely he would retreat when he reached the wall of flame that filled the third floor, wouldn't he? But what if he didn't? Judd felt a huge and terrible responsibility for his new friend and brother. He couldn't afford to lose Lionel. He would never forgive himself. He charged into that building like a crazy man, not knowing whether he was there to drag Lionel out or help him find his uncle André. All he knew was that he was on his way.

People tried to stop Judd just as they had tried to stop Lionel. But the roar of the fire grew, and soon people worried only about themselves. To Judd it seemed the heat and noise intensified with every step up the stairs. On the second-floor landing he ran into a family who seemed to be moving in slow motion. The man was huge and heavy. He waddled across the landing, his big belly leading the way, with an old woman straddling his neck and a frail, elderly man in each arm. The men howled and the woman sobbed. The man merely looked resolute, as if the only thing on his mind was saving every member of his family. Judd hesitated and watched them go. The man stumbled on the first step leading to the lower floor and had to run awkwardly downstairs to remain upright. He turned at the last moment and his shoulder crashed against the wall, making his wife scream, but he somehow kept any of the three he carried from getting hurt.

Judd turned back in time to see Lionel barging up to the third floor, where the heat and flames were so oppressive Judd couldn't imagine how anyone could breathe, let alone survive. His instincts screamed at him to turn back, but he would not let Lionel do this alone.

When Judd finally caught up with him on the third-floor landing, Lionel had stopped at last. The fire billowed, flames devouring the ceiling, popping bulbs and melting fixtures. Old drywall and slats burned and fell around them. "We can't go any further!" Judd hollered, but Lionel either didn't hear or refused to pay attention.

"He's right through there!" Lionel screamed, pointing at the first door across the hall. The door seemed the only thing above floor level not on fire. "LeRoy would never have had time to lock him in!"

"That knob will be hot!" Judd said, but Lionel was ahead of him, pulling off his shirt and wrapping his hand in it. He ducked and scampered to the door, turning the knob while Judd kicked at the door.

The knob was so hot it started Lionel's shirt afire. He beat it out on his thigh as the door swung open and banged against the wall. There was no doubt the fire had begun in this room, and LeRoy—if he had done it—had not even tried to hide the evidence. A five-gallon gas can lay in a corner, sending flames licking to the ceiling.

Judd had never felt such heat, and it

seemed as if his skin were blistering and might slide right off his face.

"Here he is!" Lionel shouted from the bathroom. "He's bleeding!"

Judd caught himself just in time to keep from telling Lionel not to try to move André. How absurd would that be? No matter what André's injuries, even tossing him out the window would be preferable to letting him roast to death in this room.

Judd made his way to the bathroom door, where Lionel had already begun dragging his uncle out by his shoulders. Judd was bigger and stronger than Lionel, so he told Lionel to grab André's feet. Judd thrust his fists under André's arms from behind and began scooting backward out of the bathroom and toward the door.

Praying they would have time to get the man down the stairs before the whole building came crashing around them, Judd heard sirens and people screaming. He was suddenly aware that his left forearm was being drenched anew with every beat of André's heart.

"At least he's still alive!" Judd shouted.

EIGHT

Hard Truth

THOUGH André was not a big man, he was barely conscious and unable to help Lionel and Judd get him down two flights of stairs. Judd thought André was trying to talk, but all he could hear was a gurgle above the roar of the flames and the crashing of his own heart.

Judd tried to keep his eyes closed because the heat and smoke grated on them. He peeked each time he felt Lionel backing into another turn, and once he saw a burning wood slat drop onto Lionel's shoulder. Lionel flinched when it hit him, but when it stuck and kept burning, he had to drop one of André's legs to brush it away. That made Judd lose his grip, and he fought to hang on. André's weight carried Judd down toward André, and he found himself nearly stumbling over the wounded man.

As the boys struggled to get a new hold on André, a great roar and crash came from above them, and Judd knew the top floor was giving way. Would it take the second floor with it and crush them beneath a fiery load? They didn't have time to wonder. With his skin blistering and his lungs desperate for clear air, Judd thrust his hands deeper under André's arms, lifted, and began moving as quickly as he knew how. He tried to keep as much weight as possible off Lionel, who was lighter and lower on the stairs, trying to guide their cargo to safety.

André thrashed and screamed, and Judd wondered if he would have to punch him in the face to protect him from himself, the way he had seen in movies. But there was no time, and he didn't know if he was strong enough to knock out a grown man anyway.

Fire surrounded the boys, and Judd heard the walls and ceiling dropping behind him. The whole staircase shuddered beneath their weight, and as the last of the other tenants pushed through the front door and out into the night, three firemen swept in, axes in hand, and surveyed the scene.

They apparently didn't see Judd and Lionel and André at first. They studied the crumbling holocaust, looked at each other, shook their heads, and turned to head back out.

"Hey!" Judd shrieked. "Help us!"

The three whirled as one, tossed their axes out through the glass doors, and rushed up the stairs. "You boys get out now!" the first said. "We've got this guy!"

Judd let go of André, who now rested awkwardly with his head upstairs and his feet in Lionel's hands. Lionel refused to let go. Judd kept the front door in sight, fearing he would pass out if he didn't get fresh air, and right now. He grabbed Lionel on the way past and was amazed at how strong the younger boy was. Judd could barely budge him at first, but with his weight heading down, he got enough leverage and yanked Lionel away from his uncle.

Just as the first fireman lifted André and threw him over his shoulder, the whole staircase dropped three feet. That made the firemen and the boys fall onto the burning floor, and André dropped onto his back. "Get out! Get out!" the first fireman yelled. "All of you!"

He lifted André again and used his knees and shoulders to herd the boys the last few feet to the door. At a dead run now, the big man carried the thrashing André on his back. He charged through what was left of the glass, Judd and Lionel a step ahead of him. The four of them tumbled and rolled out into the night air, landing in a heap in the grass. Judd sucked in the sweet air for his very life.

The fireman dragged André thirty feet from the inferno and laid him on his back, barking into his radio for paramedics. He whirled to face the building and, not seeing his coworkers, sprinted back, grabbing his axe on the way. Judd watched him call for support, frantic to get to the two firemen still trapped inside.

As more firemen donned oxygen masks and began the dangerous journey into the fire, Judd turned back to see Lionel sprawled nearly atop his uncle, who appeared to be breathing his last. Blood still spurted from the right side of his neck, but his heartbeat had slowed and weakened. "No! No!" Lionel screamed. "God, don't let him die! André!"

Judd covered with his hand the deep wound in André's neck as the man tried to talk. "This is what hell will be like," he rasped. "I deserve it, Lionel."

"No! We all deserve it, André! But you don't have to go! Don't go!"

"It's too late for me. I'm not gonna make it, boy."

"André! You can still go to heaven! Pray! Pray!"

"It's too late."

"It wasn't too late for the thief on the cross! Please, André!"

Judd's fingers were directly on the carotid artery, which is where Judd assumed André had been shot before the apartment was set afire. He felt precisely when André's heart stopped. André thrashed a bit more, shaking his head. "Can't breathe," he whispered. And suddenly he went rigid.

Lionel sobbed while using his shirttail to wipe André's face and his own mouth. He leaned over and began mouth-to-mouth resuscitation, but Judd knew the heartbeat was as important as the breathing. Judd began rhythmically pushing on André's chest, and with each thrust a tiny rivulet of blood eked from André's neck.

"It's no use, Lionel," Judd said. "He's gone."

"No! Don't give up!"

Two medics arrived and pulled the boys off André. "Let me get in here, guys," one said. "I can do more than you can."

He slapped an oxygen mask on André as his partner felt for a pulse in the neck. "What happened to this guy?" he said.

"I think he was shot," Judd said.

"Keep him alive!" Lionel insisted.

"It's too late, son. I'm sorry."

"Try!"

"Son, this man is gone. Now we have firemen to attend to. I'm sorry."

Lionel was inconsolable. He would not leave André's body, even when the medics came back and covered it with a sheet and told Lionel someone would be there soon for the body. Judd tried to get Lionel to come with him back to the car, but he would not budge. He didn't talk, didn't pray, didn't do anything but kneel next to André, rocking and shaking his head as he wept.

"I'm going to go tell Vicki and Ryan what happened and bring the car back to get you," Judd said. Lionel didn't respond. "I'll be back as soon as I can, but I'm probably not going to be able to park very close. You don't have to come until someone comes for André, OK?" Judd got no reaction from Lionel. "I'll be right back," he said.

Judd planned to jog back to the car, but when he rose, he could barely walk. He didn't know what he had done to strain his ankles, his knees, his hips, even his shoulders. He felt like an old man, slowly making his way past the tenants, the onlookers, and the emergency vehicles. The cool night air felt good in his lungs, but it stung his face, which he was afraid to touch. He knew he would have blisters and burns, but he was sure he had not been seriously or permanently injured.

The farther Judd got from the burning building, the stranger the experience seemed. Was this a dream? Had it really happened? He couldn't imagine anything as traumatic as losing his family to the Rapture and being left behind, but neither had he ever been through something like this. The sounds of the blaze faded more with each step, and though he saw the shadows of the flames in the darkness, he had to turn and look once more to let the reality set in.

Judd began to pray. He felt sobs rising in his chest as he thanked God that LeRoy, or whoever had done this, had not arrived while Lionel was still in that apartment. Surely he too would have been shot and burned to death.

Lionel had tried so hard to reach his uncle for God. Judd could only hope that Lionel would eventually accept that these decisions were personal. After all, that was why both he and Lionel had been left behind in the first place. No one could make the decision for them.

The police had already barricaded several streets leading to the apartment fire. Gawkers seemed to come from everywhere. Judd finally decided he couldn't cater to his fatigue and pain anymore. He owed it to Vicki and to Ryan to get to them and tell them how much longer he would be.

But when he got to where he had left them in the car, he found nothing. Now what? Neither of them was old enough to drive. Had someone stolen the car? If so, where were Vicki and Ryan? Had LeRoy come by here?

Judd spun around in the street, his eyes landing on a cop directing traffic away from the fire. The cop was short and husky with thick, wavy blond hair. "Someone stole my car!" Judd shouted. "And two of my friends were in it!"

"So *they* stole it," the cop said. "Find them, you find your car."

"They're both too young to drive."

"Then find 'em quick. I'm kinda busy here."

"I have no idea where to look."

The cop talked without looking at Judd, keeping his attention on the traffic. "What kind of a car was it?"

"A BMW."

The cop laughed. "Daddy's car, hmm?"

"Yup."

"And what was a nice boy like you doing in a neighborhood like this with a car like that?"

"Looking out for a friend."

"Another rich kid with no business here?"

"Not exactly."

"Can't help you, son. 'Fraid lost or even stolen cars are pretty low priority these days. We barely had enough guys to handle this fire."

"If I tell you who firebombed that building and murdered a guy, will you help me find my car?"

The cop suddenly focused on Judd. "You're serious, aren't you?"

"I couldn't be more serious," he said.

"Wait right there," the cop said. He hurried to the side of the street and dragged into the intersection an oversized, blue wooden construction horse with "Police Line. Do Not Cross" painted on it in white. He stepped to his squad car and spoke into his radio. Then he waved Judd over. His nameplate read Sgt. Thomas Fogarty.

"That'll take care of the traffic until I get some backup," he said. "Now, listen—whew, you smell like you were in that fire."

"I was," Judd said, eager to tell his story.

Sergeant Fogarty grabbed Judd by the shirt and pushed him up against a light pole. "You listen to me, kid. This has nothing to do with you, but I was in the homicide division until I got busted back down to traffic detail for reasons you don't need to know. I tell you that only so you'll know that I understand murder. I'm not lookin' to crack some new case to get back into homicide, but that wouldn't be bad either. The thing is, if you know anything about this fire and it really involves a murder, I'll know whether you're lying or if there's a ring of truth to it. Now what's your name?"

Judd told him and showed him his driver's license. "How long you been drivin'?" Fogarty asked.

"Not that long," Judd said.

Fogarty directed Judd to the squad car, where they sat in the front seat. The cop radioed in a request for an APB (all points bulletin) on Judd's car. Then Judd told him the whole story. He began with losing his family in the vanishings ("I lost a few relatives myself," Fogarty said) and told how he and Lionel had met. He told the cop about the phony suicide/murder, the invasion of Lionel's home, Ryan's close call, Lionel's visit to André that evening, and everything that followed.

"So you're guessing this LeRoy is the shooter because your friend, what's his name—?"

"Ryan."

"Right, Ryan ID'd the yellow and brown van."

"Right."

"Let's get you back over to the scene and see if we can help your friend and be sure the body is taken care of."

As Sergeant Fogarty pulled out into traffic his radio squawked to life with the news that a cruiser had just pulled over the BMW that was the subject of the APB. "Who's the driver?" Fogarty asked.

"Female Caucasian, Byrne, Victoria, underage, no license. Other occupant male Caucasian, Daley, Ryan, age twelve."

"Ten-four. What's their story?"

"She says they were awaiting two other friends, the driver, male Caucasian, Thompson, Judd Jr., sixteen, and male African-American, Washington, Lionel, thirteen. Long story, Sarge. She thought they were safe with the doors locked and engine idling. Claims they were nearly hit by a van."

"Let me guess. It was yellow and brown."

"Ten-four."

"That checks out. Don't cite her unless there's some obvious violation."

"She wasn't moving when I found her. Nothing to cite."

"Give me your ten-twenty, and I'll bring the driver within the hour."

André's body was being loaded into an ambulance when Sergeant Fogarty pulled up to the scene. He asked a paramedic to check for a carotid artery wound. "Already checked, sir. In our opinion, it was the cause of death. That'll have to be confirmed by the coroner, of course, but this man bled to death. No ID on him, by the way."

"Let me give you one," Fogarty said. He got the information from Judd and Lionel, who sat sullenly in the backseat of the squad car, and the medic pinned the identification to the body.

"It'll be like looking for a needle in a haystack," Fogarty told the boys as he drove them back to Judd's car, "but we'll use heavy duty metal detectors to try to find the bullet, and maybe the weapon, in the rubble."

Judd sighed heavily, feeling every ache and pain and grieving with Lionel, who cried softly in the backseat.

NINE

The Setup

EARLY the next morning, Judd stood gingerly in the shower, his scalp and face and neck and hands stinging from the spray on his tender flesh. If everybody else in his house had slept like he did, they had been dead to the world. What a night that had been!

All the way home, Ryan and Vicki had told and retold their harrowing escape from LeRoy and his brown and yellow van. Lionel had listened but did not respond at first. "Are you sure it was LeRoy?" Judd had asked.

"Positive," Vicki said. "Ryan got a clear look at him. We were just sitting there when we heard someone race up behind us. I was sitting behind the wheel, just to see what it felt like, and the engine was running. I had driven my friends' cars before, you know, like in an empty parking lot late at night, so I knew the basics. Anyway, we see this van come barreling past us, and we both lean up against the window for a closer look."

"Which was really stupid," Ryan said. "Especially for me. I mean, LeRoy doesn't know this car or Vicki, but he must have seen me staring at him out of the backseat. He slides to a stop and lowers the window and stares right at me. I slid off the seat and onto the floor. I said, 'Vicki, get me outta here!'"

Vicki picked up the story. "I shifted into drive and floored it, but I forgot to turn. We were on the side of the street, so I had to slam on the brakes to keep from hitting one of those, you know, utility poles. LeRoy pulled right in behind me to pin me in, but when he got out of the van, I just shifted into reverse and backed into the van. That's why your taillights are both smashed. Sorry. Anyway, he jumped back and screamed and swore at us, and I just yanked the wheel to the left, shifted again, and took off. He chased us all over the place, but I finally lost him. I was scared to death."

"He knew you could put him in that neighborhood where the murder and the arson happened," Judd said. "He *wanted* you dead. Probably still does."

"If I'd known that," Vicki said, "I probably would have been too scared to move."

"And you wouldn't be here right now," Lionel said finally. "LeRoy's a murdering scumbag. I know he'll kill me as soon as he finds me."

"He won't find you," Judd said. "He has no idea where I live, and we're keeping this car in the garage once we get home."

"I don't much care anymore," Lionel said.

Vicki turned in her seat to face him. "What do you mean?"

"I failed André," he said.

"So you want to die too?"

"Why not?"

"Because we love you," she said. "That's why. We need you in this family. I feel awful for you and sorry for your uncle, but from what you tell me, he knew the truth and had every chance to accept Christ."

As Judd stood in the shower now, he recalled Lionel's shrugging and turning away. But Judd hoped the truth of what Vicki said would settle in on Lionel this morning and that he would realize that Judd and Ryan—yes, even Ryan—felt the same way about Lionel.

Toweling off was an ordeal, because his raw burns stung. He applied petroleum jelly as Sergeant Fogarty had suggested. Judd looked forward to their ten o'clock appointment. The officer was coming to his house to talk to all of them about the next step.

"I don't feel like meeting with the cop," Lionel told Judd in the kitchen a few minutes later.

"Why not? You're going to be the key to whatever he wants to do. You're the one who knows who these people are and what's really happened."

"I don't know," Lionel said, hunched over a bowl of cereal he had not touched. "I don't feel like much of anything right now."

"You want to call Bruce? I can run you over to the church."

"Nah. I got to work this out for myself. I think I've had enough of talking with adults. First it was André, then Bruce, then LeRoy and the other guy, then Talia, then André again, and now this cop."

"Fogarty."

"Yeah."

"You shouldn't really put André or Talia in the same category as Bruce, should you?"

"I don't know what I think anymore. To tell you the truth, Judd, this makes no sense to me. Why did both André and me get second chances, but I was the only one who did anything about it?"

Judd shrugged. "You're askin' the wrong guy, Lionel. I never thought about stuff like this until last week. You're asking now like you wish André had been saved and you hadn't."

"That's sort of how I feel."

"That sounds pretty biblical to me."

"Biblical?"

"Like the way Jesus feels."

"He wants to be dead?"

"He was willing to die so we wouldn't have to die for our sins. Sounds like you wish you could have died in André's place."

"Yeah, but mostly I want to die because I messed up and André missed his chance."

"You didn't mess up, Lionel. I hate to say it, but André messed up. There was nothing more you could do. You explained. You pleaded with him. Plus, he knew all this from the beginning. He was raised the same way you were."

Lionel sat before his full bowl, hands in his lap, head down. Silent.

Sergeant Thomas Fogarty of the Chicago Police Department showed up that morning in a late-model sports car and street clothes. "We have a bit of a problem," he said as Judd showed him to a chair in the living room.

Judd sat across from him, Vicki on the couch, Lionel on the floor against the wall, Ryan stretched out on the carpet.

Fogarty turned to Lionel. "Son, ironically, your uncle's body was taken to the same morgue the first murder victim was taken to. Of course the identification you gave me, and which we put with the body, ran into a duplicate record on their computer. I explained the situation to the medical examiner's office, so they have André Dupree correctly identified this time. But now they want to exhume the body of the first André Dupree. You know what that means?"

"Dig him up?"

"Right, to do another autopsy, this time with murder in mind."

"Why is that a problem?" Judd asked.

"That's not the problem. I don't know when or how they'll do that or what they'll do with any new evidence they uncover. Our problem is caseload and jurisdiction."

"What's that?" Ryan asked.

"Because we're still trying to dig out from all the problems associated with the disappearances, everybody on the police force is already working overtime every day. We have to set priorities."

"And murder isn't a priority?" Judd said.

Sergeant Fogarty looked uncomfortable.

"This is not easy to say," he said, "especially in this day and age. But we have to face the facts. Prejudice is still alive and well, even among the police. Sometimes especially among the police."

"What are you saying?" Vicki asked.

"Here's the thing. I spent most of last night talking to my old boss in Homicide. I told him the whole story, and he thinks there's a good chance we can nail this LeRoy Banks for both murders—André and the André look-alike. As long as LeRoy is living here in Mount Prospect, that's where the jurisdiction problem comes in. The Chicago PD often cooperates—in a manner of speaking—with suburban departments, but here's where, unfortunately, the racism surfaces.

"My boss claims he was speaking for *his* bosses, but I think I know him better than that. He was speaking his own mind and pretending he wasn't."

Lionel leaned forward. "What'd he say?"

Fogarty pursed his lips and shook his head, as if he could hardly bring himself to repeat it. "He said to me, 'Tommy, with everything we've got on our plates right now, everybody overworked and all, people are asking themselves what do they care about this element killing each other off.'"

"I have no idea what you just said," Ryan said, sitting up.

"I do," Lionel said. "Nobody cares if blacks kill blacks. Especially if they're lowlifes like LeRoy and my uncle and whoever that first victim was."

"That's exactly right," Fogarty said.

"So, you're not going to help us?" Lionel said.

"If I wasn't going to try, I wouldn't be here," the cop said. "I'm a police officer because I'm a justice freak. The problem is, I represent the Chicago PD, and LeRoy Banks is living too far from home right now. I'd have to somehow get Banks back into Chicago."

"Because otherwise, your people don't care enough," Lionel said.

"I'm afraid that's right."

"So what do we do now?"

"You understand I can only advise you," Fogarty said. "I can't do anything for you or with you, and I have no official capacity outside Chicago."

Judd and Vicki nodded. Lionel turned his face away. Ryan still seemed puzzled.

"Our people know of Banks and think we can link him to other killings. But as long as he's holed up this far from Chicago—"

"And nobody down there cares enough," Lionel interrupted.

"—Right, that too. I think your best chance is to scare him out of your house and get him to set up shop back in Chicago where he belongs. Then he's out of your hair, and he becomes Chicago's problem."

"But they don't care," Lionel said, "and when he finds out I've moved back home, he comes back and wipes me out."

"Oh, I wouldn't move back there if I were you," Fogarty said. "Even if you get him to move out. At least until you hear he's been caught and charged."

"So until then, he wins."

"Exactly."

"I'm for trying to run him off," Lionel said. "But how do we do that?"

"That I cannot tell you," Fogarty said. "I have some ideas about how someone might, how shall we say it, persuade someone to move on. But one thing I must caution you: Don't ever confront him in person. You know already that he's armed and dangerous. He'd just as soon kill you as to look at you. He's done it, and he'd do it again. You already know he knows Lionel was with André just before he got there. And he knows Ryan and Vicki were in the neighborhood."

"I'm the only one who's never seen him or been seen by him," Judd said.

"Unless he saw you when he came racing out of the alley last night," Lionel said.

"I doubt it," Judd said.

"I wouldn't risk it," Lionel said.

"Neither would I," Fogarty said. "But I'll tell you what I will do. I'm going to investigate this story and these two murders on my own time. When I get enough evidence on LeRoy, I'm going to be looking for him in his old neighborhood. If you can spook him to the point where he will retreat to there, even one more time, I'll stop him for any reason I can think of. If he so much as has a broken taillight or a loud muffler, I'll pull him over and find a reason to take him to the precinct station house. Once there, I'll find a way to fingerprint him, interview him about two mysterious deaths, and start working on getting him off the streets."

"I believe he's already murdered the guy André told me about and, of course, André," Lionel said.

"Assuming you're right on those, that makes at least four."

"Four?"

"Didn't you see the paper today? Two of the firemen who went into that building last night never made it out. If that was arson—and they found the source of the fire, a gas can, in an apartment rented under the name Cornelius Grey—deaths related to it can be considered homicides. Mr. Grey hasn't been seen there for a long time, and we know he was not the murder victim. But Grey *is* a known associate of LeRoy Banks."

"Connie Grey is an associate of LeRoy's all right," Lionel said, sounding angry. "He's livin' in my house with his sister, Talia."

Fogarty was speedily taking notes. "So LeRoy Banks and Cornelius Grey are the two kingpins of the little group that moved into your house."

Lionel nodded.

"And Talia is Grey's sister."

Lionel nodded again.

"Grey hasn't been tied into any of this before," Fogarty said. "Wonder what's become of him?"

"He's the quiet one of those two," Lionel said. "I don't know if it means anything, but André always kind of liked him. André hated LeRoy. Said he was a bully, a big mouth, a know-it-all. Liked to intimidate people."

"Liked to do more than that to them," Fogarty said. "Now let me just think out loud here about how I might encourage illegal squatters—you know what that means?"

"People who move into a place they don't own?"

"Yeah. Here's what a person might do to get them to move on. . . ."

For the next hour, Judd took notes. Tom Fogarty told story after story of pranks, ruses, and tricks that had worked on stubborn cases. His favorite was the time the police sent notices to several known felons, informing them they had won expensive gifts, prizes, and trips in a special sweepstakes. All they had to do was come to the ballroom of a swanky downtown hotel to claim them. About 80 percent of the targets of the sting showed up and, at the appropriate and surprising instant, were arrested on their outstanding warrants.

That wasn't something Judd and his friends could pull off without a lot of money and help, but several others of Fogarty's suggestions seemed right up their alley.

TEN

The Sting

IT FELL to Judd, who believed he was the only one of the four kids who had never been seen by LeRoy Banks, to keep an eye on Lionel's house. Fortunately, his mother's minivan was also in the garage, and he was able to use that and not risk LeRoy recognizing the car that had backed into his brown and yellow monstrosity a few nights before.

The first couple of days Judd tooled around the neighborhood, occasionally passing Lionel's house. The only thing he noticed was that nothing seemed to be going on. He saw neither the old van nor the roadster Lionel had told him about. Maybe LeRoy was lying low for a while, more concerned about keeping out of sight than trying to eliminate the one person who could implicate him in the arson and murders: Lionel.

Finally, though, Judd caught a break. He saw the old brown and yellow van, only it didn't look so old anymore, and it wasn't brown and yellow. It had been spruced up, the rust spots filled and the whole thing painted a muted cream. It looked pretty good. Judd checked in with Sergeant Fogarty, who found out that LeRoy had ordered new plates too. They were for an off-white van in Talia Grey's name, but Fogarty said the van had the same vehicle ID number as LeRoy's. What had not changed, however, were all the city stickers on the far right side of the front windshield. That was the one thing Judd remembered from the van that flashed so close to him in the alley the weekend before. At first all he had seen were the headlights. At the last moment that windshield came into view for the shortest instant, and Judd remembered wondering where in the world they would put another sticker.

When he saw the "new" van, it all came back to him. Someone had had the nerve to park the thing right in front of Lionel's house, as usual. Eventually they would have to get a Mount Prospect city sticker. On the other hand, Judd knew, that would be the last priority of the local police department. If the Chicago PD didn't even care to investigate suspicious deaths in the black community, Mount Prospect might let a few delinquent city stickers slide during a season of international chaos.

Judd could only wonder what type of trouble Talia had been in with LeRoy when LeRoy found out she had borrowed his roadster and taken Lionel, of all people, to see André. Clearly, it seemed LeRoy was intent on doing away with anyone who knew anything about the first murder. That likely included Lionel.

Judd hadn't seen Talia while staking out the area, but one day something showed up on the front porch that made Judd squint, shake his head, and wonder. It was a duffel bag with Lionel's name on it, plain as day. Someone had set it on the top step. To normal passersby, perhaps it wouldn't even catch their attention. But to Judd, and to anyone who knew Lionel and his situation, this seemed some kind of a signal.

Judd drove to a nearby elementary school, closed since the disappearances, and parked in the deserted staff lot. He then walked idly through the neighborhood, passing Lionel's house on the other side of the street. He still had seen no occupants of the home in all the time he had spent spying on it, but that bag and that repainted van meant someone had to be there.

That evening he mentioned the bag to Lionel.

"That's the bag I used to take on my sports and Y trips," he said. "I thought it was stuffed way deep in my closet. I have no idea what it means. I want to see it."

"I suppose if we go at night we'll be safe," Judd said. "Anybody else want to go?"

"Not me," Ryan said.

"I thought you were getting brave on us all of a sudden," Lionel said. "Don't fall back to being a chicken now."

"I'm not! But I don't care if I never get chased by a van again—I don't care what color it is—as long as I live."

"I'm not afraid of the van," Lionel said. "But I wouldn't want to run into LeRoy right now."

"I want to go," Vicki said, "but I want to stay out of sight until we know no one is watching us."

"Promise," Judd said. "That'll go for you too, Lionel."

"Yeah, I guess I'd be pretty conspicuous in my own neighborhood when everyone knows I don't live there anymore."

"I'm stayin' here," Ryan repeated.

"It's all right with me," Judd said. "As long as you think you'll be all right alone."

"I'll feel safer here. Anyway, like I said, I'm

not a chicken anymore. I just don't want to push my luck too far with those murderers."

"I can't blame you," Judd said. "Let's go."

Judd left Ryan with the car phone number, just in case. Several minutes later, with Vicki ducking down in the front passenger seat and Lionel lying out of sight across the backseat of the minivan, Judd drove past Lionel's house. "What do you see?" Lionel wanted to know.

"Nothing. Not a thing. I mean nothing on the porch anyway. The cream van is out front, and there's a light on in a back room."

"That's where Ryan said he heard Talia talking on the phone the other day," Lionel said. "I wonder how she feels about André."

"Wait," Judd said. "I just saw someone! It's a woman, and she's coming from that back room into the hall. The light just went out in that room and on in the hall."

"Park somewhere!" Lionel said. "I want to see if it's Talia."

Judd pulled off to the side, several houses past Lionel's. "You see anybody on the street?" Lionel asked. "Can I sit up?"

"Yeah, but don't do anything stupid."

Lionel sat up. "What, like jumping out of the car and telling everyone in the neighborhood I've come home? Whoa! I can't see anything from here. Back up closer to my house."

"I don't think that's smart," Judd said. "We're going to start drawing attention to ourselves if we do a lot of moving back and forth."

"Then I'm going to sneak up closer and get a look through the window."

"No you're not!" Vicki said, sitting up herself. "We came close enough to losing you the other night. What if LeRoy or Cornelius or whatever his name is in there?"

"Why don't we find out?" Lionel said.

"Not by going up to the house!" Judd said.

"Let's call 'em," Lionel said.

Judd and Vicki looked at each other. "We need to keep this phone open for Ryan," Judd said.

"Ryan will be fine for a few minutes," Vicki said. "No one there will recognize my voice. How about I call?"

"Do it!" Lionel said.

Judd showed her how to dial.

"What if they have caller ID?" Vicki said.

"They don't," Lionel said. "It's my phone, and we don't have it. Unless they added it, and why would they?"

"Even if they do, it's going to trace to this mobile phone," Judd said. "And there's no way the mobile phone company will give out any information on the number. Even if they did, it's listed under my mom's name. Those guys wouldn't have a clue."

"Shh!" Vicki said. "It's ringing."

Judd told her to leave the phone in the cradle so the speakerphone would come on. A female voice answered.

"Who am I speaking to?" Vicki asked.

"Who's askin'?"

"That's Talia!" Lionel mouthed.

"A friend," Vicki said.

"A friend of who?"

"André."

"Oh, oh!" Talia wailed. "Who is this? You know he's dead, don't you? Started a fire, shot himself, and burned himself up in a fire the other night."

"Who told you that?" Vicki said.

"A friend of his."

"The same friend who gave him the gasoline?"

"What're you talking about? Who is this?"

"Someone who knows you were with André before he died."

Silence.

"Are you there, Talia?"

"How do you know my name?"

"I told you. I'm a friend. A friend of a friend. A friend you've been looking for and trying to communicate with."

"I'm going to hang up now."

"Wait! Don't! Don't you want to talk to Lionel?"

"Yes! Put him on."

"I'm here, Talia. What'd you put my duffel bag out for?"

"You saw that? Oh, thank God! Ooh, boy, I got in trouble for that. Connie come flyin' in here in LeRoy's roadster and saw that bag before I got a chance to get rid of it, and he told LeRoy. My own brother, tellin' on me. LeRoy liked to kill me."

"The way he did André."

"LeRoy didn't kill André!"

"'Course he did, Talia. You were there with me. You know André didn't have any five gallons of gas. And if he wanted to kill himself, why did he have to set a fire?"

"LeRoy went to see him later that night, Lionel. Said he found him shot and his place burning."

"It's a lie and you know it. LeRoy did it, don't you see? My friend and I heard a shot and an explosion. We saw the fire and went back. LeRoy almost ran us over in the van. Why do you think he got it painted? Huh? My friend and I dragged André out of there, but it was too late. LeRoy shot him in the neck, blew open some kind of artery—"

"Carotid," Judd whispered.

"Yeah, the carotid artery."

"I don't want to hear this."

"'Course you don't. Truth hurts. You loved André. I know you did. I loved him too. That's why we have to face the truth."

Judd and the others heard Talia crying.

"Why did you want me to see my duffel bag?" Lionel asked.

"I just wanted you not to come around here for a while. LeRoy's been blamin' you for André, shootin' himself. Says it must've been something you said when you saw him. He knew I wouldn't upset André, but he was mad at me for goin' anyway, and especially for taking you."

"You've got to get away from LeRoy," Lionel said. "He's bad news."

"I know," she said. "You know what LeRoy wants to do now? He wants to see if there's any insurance on Connie's apartment that burned, or any life insurance on André."

"You're kidding."

"It's true. They're acting all sad about André and all, but LeRoy and Connie both are talking about checking into some kind of insurance payoff."

"That's sick. Anyway, André never had any life insurance, as far as I knew."

"LeRoy thought he might have had some through his work, you know, before he got laid off from the city."

"Why didn't he try to get that when it looked like André had killed himself before?"

"He was going to. Said he was gonna split it with André and the rest of us. But then he found out you were nosing around and he figured you told somebody that that wasn't André's body."

"I didn't."

"I know. But he didn't know that then. But that was for sure André the other night, wasn't it?"

"For sure."

"So, LeRoy's going after the money."

"How's he going to do that?"

"Call the landlord I guess. Or the city about the life insurance."

"Sick."

"I know. Anyway, stay away from here for a while. I'm sure glad you saw my message. And I sure hope you're wrong about LeRoy."

Lionel shook his head and said his good-byes. Judd called Sergeant Fogarty on the way home. There had to be a way to use LeRoy Banks' greed against himself.

"I have an idea," Judd told Fogarty. "I want to come downtown and tell you about it."

"I'll meet you halfway," Fogarty said, and he set the meeting at an all-night restaurant in Des Plaines.

By the end of their meeting, it was clear to

Judd that Fogarty liked what he heard. "I took you for a sharp kid," the cop said, "but who knew you had a mind like that? Let's hope you always use it for the right side of the law."

"Oh, I will," Judd said. They laid their plans, and on the way back home to Mount Prospect, Judd smiled at the thought that, just a few weeks before, he was using for his own gain the brain Tom Fogarty admired so much.

The next day, while Judd coached Vicki on what to say over the phone, he knew what Tom Fogarty was doing. After assuring his bosses that he would deliver a known killer right into their hands within a block of the precinct station house, Tom would run a few errands. He would rent a storefront office, move in some rented furniture, have his name painted on the window, "Thomas M. Fogarty, Attorney at Law," and would wait there for one LeRoy Banks to present himself.

When Judd got the call from Sergeant Fogarty that everything was in place, the cop told him of his own bit of creativity. "I set up a messy secretary's desk all covered with work and a cardboard sign that says, 'In the law library. Back in 30 minutes.'"

"Perfect," Judd said. "Talia tells us LeRoy will be home late morning. I'll let you know when to expect him."

At eleven-thirty the four kids finished a prayer meeting, piled into Judd's minivan, and drove to Ryan's house. The plan was to call LeRoy from there, just in case he grew suspicious and tried to trace the call.

Ryan let them in, and he and Lionel and Judd sat quietly while Vicki dialed. She threw on a very adult-sounding voice. Cornelius Grey answered the phone.

"Mr. Grey, this is Maria Diablo from the law offices of Thomas Fogarty in Chicago. Mr. Fogarty is representing the insurance company handling the settlements in the destruction by fire of your apartment building last week."

"Yeah, what do we get?"

"Well, sir, I'm not at liberty to discuss the amount over the phone, but I can tell you it is substantial. Unfortunately, the payout must go to the payer of the rent over the last several months, and our records indicate that it has not been you."

"No, the rent's been paid lately by a friend of mine, helpin' me out. Name is LeRoy Banks."

"Would I be able to speak to him?"

"Sure!"

Judd and the others heard Cornelius Grey quickly filling in LeRoy on their huge stroke of luck. "Let me have that phone," LeRoy said, clearly doubtful.

"Who is this?" he demanded.

Vicki went through the same routine with him, in its entirety, just the way Judd had scripted it. Rather than let LeRoy build on his doubts, she made the prize a little harder to get.

"Of course, sir, we would not be able to issue a check of this magnitude unless you were able to prove to us that you are the same LeRoy Banks who has been paying the rent on Cornelius Grey's apartment."

"Oh, I'll be able to prove it all right. What time did you say Mr. Fogarty could see me?"

On the way back to Judd's house, Lionel and Ryan congratulated Judd for his idea and Vicki for her performance. When they arrived, Judd went to call Sergeant Fogarty to fill him in on how things went. Not only did he want to tell Fogarty when to expect to see LeRoy Banks and Cornelius Grey, but he also wanted to beg to be there himself to see the big arrest. It was only fair that Vicki be allowed to be there too, but he couldn't imagine the Chicago Police Department risking having civilians so close to what could become a dangerous situation.

Still, he would ask. He wanted above anything to see the look on LeRoy's face when he found out he was not getting a check but rather getting arrested for murder. When he reached for the phone, however, it rang.

"Are you watching channel nine?" Bruce Barnes asked Judd.

"No, we're in the middle of—"

"Turn on nine," Bruce insisted. "I've got a hunch the guy they're interviewing could be the one we're supposed to watch out for."

"You mean the Antichrist?" Judd asked, grabbing the remote control. He wanted to tell Bruce the story of the sting, but that would have to wait until he talked to Fogarty.

He thanked Bruce and turned on the television, watching in fascination. "You'd better call the sergeant," Vicki suggested.

"Yeah!" he said, turning down the volume and dialing the number.

Fogarty was ecstatic, and he wasn't closed to the idea of Judd and Vicki being there when it all happened. "We have a one-way mirror at the back where my backups will be. That's where they'll come from to surprise these two when I give the signal. I think if you two agree to stay there until it's all over, you could have a great view and stay safe. I think it'd be too risky to have your young friend there, and we don't want the murder victim's nephew in the neighborhood at all that day, just in case."

"But Vicki and I can come, really?"

"Sure. Just be sure you're an hour early and park far away."

Judd couldn't wait. As he hung up he looked at his watch and decided he and Vicki would have to leave within the hour to be downtown in time to be in place. He turned up the TV and watched more of the interview with the man Bruce now suspected could be the Antichrist.

Boy, would he and Bruce have a lot to talk about the next time they got together!

ABOUT THE AUTHORS

Jerry B. Jenkins (www.jerryjenkins.com) is the writer of the Left Behind series. He is author of more than one hundred books, of which eleven have reached the *New York Times* best-seller list. Former vice president for publishing for the Moody Bible Institute of Chicago, he also served many years as editor of *Moody* magazine and is now Moody's writer-at-large.

His writing has appeared in publications as varied as *Reader's Digest, Parade,* in-flight magazines, and many Christian periodicals. He has written books in four genres: biography, marriage and family, fiction for children, and fiction for adults.

Jenkins's biographies include books with Hank Aaron, Bill Gaither, Luis Palau, Walter Payton, Orel Hershiser, Nolan Ryan, Brett Butler, and Billy Graham, among many others.

Eight of his apocalyptic novels—*Left Behind, Tribulation Force, Nicolae, Soul Harvest, Apollyon, Assassins, The Indwelling,* and *The Mark*—have appeared on the Christian Booksellers Association's best-selling fiction list and the *Publishers Weekly* religion best-seller list. *Left Behind* was nominated for Book of the Year by the Evangelical Christian Publishers Association in 1997, 1998, 1999, and 2000. *The Indwelling* was number one on the *New York Times* best-seller list for four consecutive weeks.

As a marriage and family author and speaker, Jenkins has been a frequent guest on Dr. James Dobson's *Focus on the Family* radio program.

Jerry is also the writer of the nationally syndicated sports story comic strip *Gil Thorp,* distributed to newspapers across the United States by Tribune Media Services.

Jerry and his wife, Dianna, live in Colorado.

Dr. Tim LaHaye (www.timlahaye.com), who conceived the idea of fictionalizing an account of the Rapture and the Tribulation, is a noted author, minister, and nationally recognized speaker on Bible prophecy. He is the founder of both Tim LaHaye Ministries and The Pre-Trib Research Center. Presently Dr. LaHaye speaks at many of the major Bible prophecy conferences in the U.S. and Canada, where his nine current prophecy books are very popular.

Dr. LaHaye holds a doctor of ministry degree from Western Theological Seminary and the doctor of literature degree from Liberty University. For twenty-five years he pastored one of the nation's outstanding churches in San Diego, which grew to three locations. It was during that time that he founded two accredited Christian high schools, a Christian school system of ten schools, and Christian Heritage College.

Dr. LaHaye has written over forty books, with over 30 million copies in print in thirty-three languages. He has written books on a wide variety of subjects, such as family life, temperaments, and Bible prophecy. His current fiction works, written with Jerry Jenkins—*Left Behind, Tribulation Force, Nicolae, Soul Harvest, Apollyon, Assassins, The Indwelling,* and *The Mark*—have all reached number one on the Christian best-seller charts. Other works by Dr. LaHaye are *Spirit-Controlled Temperament; How to Be Happy Though Married; Revelation Unveiled; Understanding the Last Days; Rapture under Attack; Are We Living in the End Times?;* and the youth fiction series Left Behind: The Kids.

He is the father of four grown children and grandfather of nine. Snow skiing, waterskiing, motorcycling, golfing, vacationing with family, and jogging are among his leisure activities.